EARL LOVELACE was born in Toco, Trinidad in 1935, and spent his childhood in Tobago and Port of Spain. He first worked with the Trinidad Publishing Company, and later joined the Civil Service, serving first in the Forestry Department and then in the Department of Agriculture.

His first novel, *While Gods Are Falling*, won him the BP Independence Literary Award. It was followed by *The Schoolmaster*, a novel which drew on his experiences of rural Trinidad. The promise evident in these novels of the sixties was fulfilled in *The Dragon Can't Dance*, and *The Wine of Astonishment* which, West Africa magazine argued, 'put him in the front rank of Caribbean writers'. It was followed by a collection of plays, *Jestina's Calypso*, which was published in 1984. His latest work, *A Brief Conversion and Other Stories* groups together twelve of the author's best short stories.

Earl Lovelace lives in Trinidad where he works in the Folk Theatre and teaches creative writing at the University of the West Indies.

EARL LOVELACE

A BRIEF CONVERSION
AND OTHER STORIES

HEINEMANN

Heinemann International
a division of Heinemann Educational Books Ltd
Halley Court, Jordan Hill, Oxford OX2 8EJ

Heinemann Educational Books Inc.
361 Hanover Street, Portsmouth, New Hampshire, 03801, USA

Heinemann Educational Books (Nigeria) Ltd
PMB 5205, Ibadan
Heinemann Kenya Ltd
Kijabe Street, PO Box 45314, Nairobi
Heinemann Educational Boleswa
PO Box 10103, Village Post Office, Gaborone, Botswana
Heinemann Publishers (Caribbean) Ltd
175 Mountain View Avenue, Kingston 6, Jamaica

OXFORD   EDINBURGH   MELBOURNE
SYDNEY   AUCKLAND   SINGAPORE
MADRID   ATHENS   BOLOGNA   HARARE

First published by Heinemann International
in the Caribbean Writers Series in 1988

British Library Cataloguing in Publication Data

Lovelace, Earl, 1935–
A brief conversion & other stories.
(Caribbean writers series).
I. Title   II. Series
813[F]   PR9272.9.L6

ISBN 0–435–98882–4

Typeset by Activity Ltd.,
Salisbury, Wiltshire

Printed in Great Britain by
Cox & Wyman Ltd, Reading, Berkshire

90   91   92   93   94   10   9   8   7   6   5   4   3   2

CONTENTS

For Marjorie
and Lawrence and Jenny
and for Errol Jones

A BRIEF CONVERSION

Every third Sunday just at the hour when the Shouters are holding service in their church up on the hill into which our street disappears, a bicycle bell rings once; and with the bleak brightness of an undertaker, Mr Fitzie, itinerant barber and sweepstake seller, one of his legs shorter than the other, appears out of the clump of trees that ring our house, pushing his bicycle into our yard with his assured hip-shorted walk, a rhythmic drop-rising, up-downing, each step, climbing down from the height it would ascend with the next, prancing with the oiled inhuman smoothness of the pedal of a foot machine, sets down his box on the big stone in the shade of our chenette tree, and calls out to my mother, and she sends us out, my brother and me, with two chairs, one for Mr Fitzie to use and the other for her to sit on to be director and witness of this rite.

Of those mornings, these remain with me: the smell of the blossoms of our cedar tree, the sounds of the Shouters' hypnotic, rhythmic hymns and the clip-clipping of Mr Fitzie's barbering scissors as they helicopter over my head, not yet touching a hair, Mr Fitzie flexing his fingers, flourishing his dexterity and announcing his power over me before he brings the scissors down to engage my hair; the smell of cheap face powder and, on the ground beside my chair, the fluff of my shorn hair. Or was he shearing me of vanity? Do not learn the vanity of a muff. Do not learn the vanity of a covering of hair.

1

There is no mirror to see what is going on. I run my hand over my head. I feel the loss of hair. I plead, 'Mr Fitzie, it good now? I finish trim now! Enough hair gone now!'

'Hold yer head!' my mother commands.

Mr Fitzie grips my cheekbones with the vice of his fingers and he screws my head in the direction he wants it and bends it at the angle he requires it to stay; and his scissors clip, snip; and I am stifled by his old perspiration smell, and the sickly scent of cedar blossoms hangs in the air; and, from the space below his armpit, behind the flowering bluebells, butterflies fold their wings and settle in the sunshine of the hibiscus hedge, and in the tall elephant grass across the road, Mr Sylvestre's donkey jerks its ears to shake annoying horse-flies from its face.

'Hold your head,' Mr Fitzie grumbles, his fingers tightening on my temples; and the Shouters sing, *What a Friend We Have in Jesus*, breaking out from words to sounds, sighs, screams, groans, their singing punctuated and harmonised and juxtaposed, each individual rejoicing wail adding its tall sad brightness to the chorused sounds, drawing my mother in, her own humming martyred and remote for most of the hymn, then her voice breaking out in song when they get to the line: *Pilgrims in this Barren Land*.

I see me now, riveted to that chair, my eyes bright and round like polished buttons, 'Mr Fitzie, it good now!' as panic grips me.

'Trim him low, Mr Fitzie,' my mother breathes, her voice insistent, in it, more than a declaration of her will, an edge of –but, I must say it – spite.

'But, why, Pearl? Why you have to cut the boy hair like a Nazi for?' Aunt Irene asks as, bristling with a triumphant, buxom, intimidatory and to my way of thinking, unwarranted vexation, my mother marches into the house and I crawl sullen, humbled, to the mirror to check the exact degree of damage done to my appearance. 'Tell me, what reason it have for you to brutalise your boychild head so? I know Indian people does shave their boychild head, but, that is when their father dead. His father dead, Pearl?'

2

'You all right, yes, Irene,' my mother answers, in a voice of superior wisdom, with its timbre of doom, outraged that she should be required to given any explanation.

And Aunt Irene, lolling in the sunshine of our verandah, a dustercoat on, her hair in curlers and all her jewels on, lifts a luxurious hand, her bangles and bracelets jangling, and with the consciousness of a glamour that everybody associates with her stay in Port of Spain, says, 'Children like to look nice too. You think I could dare trim Ronnie like that?' Ronnie being her son, my cousin, who, when he comes to spend time with us in Cunaripo, wears a wrist watch, wears a sailor suit. Ronnie has his hair parted and brushed for the waves in it to show. Aunt Irene hugs Ronnie, kisses him: 'Ronnie, darling, what you want to do today?'

Ronnie wants six cents in his pocket to go down the street. He wants a bicycle to ride. 'But, your bicycle is in Port of Spain, darling,' Aunt Irene coos, soothingly, smoothening down his pouting face, her two hands coming together softly at his chin. Sometimes she talks of his deprivation at being in Cunaripo, of the ice cream cones he misses, the cinema shows, the circus that's visiting. 'Oh, and you know this weekend I was to go horse races in the Savannah with him ... Anyway, the little outing will do him good. With the sea so near to Cunaripo, at least he'll learn to swim.'

You dream of a place to go to and Ronnie has been there. You doubt him and he turns to his mother, 'Mummie, didn't you take me to the De Luxe cinema to see that Tarzan picture?' in this adult way of talking that makes my mother squirm.

Ronnie is not very athletic. In the races we run, I beat him every time; yet, when we play, he is Tarzan; he is Zorro. He has a little Zorro mask which he never lends me and, like Zorro, he has a whip with which he feels free to lash me, since in all our games Ronnie is the star boy and I am the crook. When we play stick-em-up, my shots are the ones that miss. He never misses. 'I get you!' he cries, celebrating his perfect marksmanship. 'You dead!'

If I argue, he sulks and refuses to play. I try to hold out against his unfairness; but, he knows that I am dying to play, and he waits

3

until I give in and say, okay. I learn to stumble, to hold my shoulder as I fall, pretending to be wounded only in the arm. He stands, at such times, with a cruel and triumphant grin on his face, his gun aimed dead at my head, ready to shoot me down in cold blood, should I seek to escape.

'You all right, yes, Irene,' my mother repeats, hinting not only at Aunt Irene's pampering of Ronnie, but at the pampering of herself, at her dreaming and creamed face and the langour of her stretching; for, Aunt Irene has this hoarse seductive voice filled with sighs and secret breaths and dark smoke, and she has a space between her teeth and she stretches and yawns and she puts her feet up on the bannister of the verandah and talks of men and she laughs that terrible laughter that makes the dogs bark and the hens scatter and my mother's eyes widen in alarm.

'Pearl, you too old-fashion. You too close to this cocoa estate.' For Aunt Irene's living in Port of Spain has brought her up to date, has given her a knowledge of 'life' and a wisdom about men; and she extends her coquettish charms to anything male, so that even our dog, Hitler, she treats with a warmth she doesn't extend to Flossie.

Dressed in a dustercoat, less frequently in shorts; for, Cunaripo doesn't rate the effort of her dressing up – her creamings and the rest she is here to take are all for Port of Spain – she sits on the rocking chair on our verandah, watching the turkey cocks dance, the yard cocks parade, casting an eye towards the road, where nothing exciting will happen. 'No,' as she puts it, 'nice man appear to make me put on some clothes'.

Seeing her on the verandah, the men who enter our yard, one or two of my father's friends glance up at her with almost sheepish grins, overpowered by her glamorous femaleness, too embarrassed, as they tell her 'good-evening', to look at her bare legs or to meet her eyes while she is wearing the dustercoat with its suggestion of undress. From her trips to the market, she returns with sea moss and sour sop and pawpaw and on a Sunday evening she emerges from the kitchen with a mug of creamy thick liquid, these fruit battered and swizzled and sweetened, set on a tray with glasses with ice; and she moves among us, pouring from the mug into the glasses, instructing, 'Drink this. It good for you.'

'You have a girl friend, Travey?' she asks me.

'Irene, what stupidness you putting in the boy head?' my mother enquires.

'Pearl, this is not something I have to put in his head. You think this generation waiting? You know how much girl friends Ronnie have since he going to that school in Belmont? Ronnie!' she calls, 'Ronnie!' And Ronnie who is nearby, tieing a string onto the abdomen of a dragonfly, lifts his head with his powerful and domineering sullenness.

'Ronnie, how much girl friends you have?'

The severe Ronnie cocks his head and looks at her in silent reprimand; but, he is unable to resist showing off. 'Three,' he says calmly. 'Now, Mummie, don't ask me that stupid question again.'

My mother groans; but, Aunt Irene doesn't even see a problem.

'Look at these lovely boychildren you have, Pearl! Look at them! Is out in the world they have to go. Don't let them go tame. Send them out brave, warriors with tall limbs, their lovely buttocks –'

'Irene!' my mother cautions. 'Irene!'

' ... their lovely buttocks dancing bold to make the world blink, to make them say,' and this she breathes, 'That is man! That is man! Like Alan Fortune.'

Of course none of us don't know who this Alan Fortune is; but, from the way her eyes close and her mouth curls around his name, he belongs, we're sure to Aunt Irene's Port of Spain, to the Dairies where she buys Ronnie ice cream cones, to the Savannah and the De Luxe cinema and the Princes Building Ballroom where she dances to Fitz Vaughn Bryan and John Buddy Williams, dressed, of course, in the latest fashion which she feels compelled to model on the stage of our verandah, just to show my mother, 'Just to show you, Pearl, the dress that I kill them with, the outfit that mash up everybody.'

5

'That is why I give Ronnie the best I can afford, if only for him to look nice. Let them go, Pearl. Let the boys go. Like lions with their manes. Like cocks with their strut and their colours. With the crown of hair on their head. The world belongs to them.'

'To them? The world?' My mother's chuckle is a groan.

'And why not, Pearl? Why not?'

'You all right, yes, Irene,' she begins disdainfully. But, the enormity of Aunt Irene's claim reaches her. She stops. She faces her sister, 'Irene, you think these boys is Ronnie? You think I could let *these lions* loose with their manes?'

It was as if my mother not only had reasons to believe that the world would be gentler with Ronnie, but, was convinced that me and my brother, unknown even to ourselves, carried in our person some more splendid and provoking quality that, without restriction, would be too much for the world to accept; so, she saw her duty as taming the warrior in us, buttoning down the challenge that, with our own innocence and carelessness, she was sure would steal through our ordinary gestures and provoke the trouble she dreaded from the world.

So maybe it was something less simple than her spite. Maybe my mother's rage and pain derived from having to tame in us what she would have loved to see us exalt, at having to send forth camouflaged as clowns the warriors she had birthed. With her voice ranging over the sounds waves make at every tide, their roarings and their sighs, she had her boychildren shorn, zugged and greased down; and she never allowed us to leave the house without the parting command, 'Button up your shirt!' Button up your shirt! As if our beauty was an insolence to be corrected, our spirit a hazard that endangered us.

'Button up your shirt, Travey!' Louder, if my father happened to be present, as if unable to resist deflecting unto him some portion of some blame, of some shame, they both knew of, making him witness to a powerlessness which she saw him as the one to correct, daring him, man that he was, if he was man, to come to my assistance so that she would be able to restate what sounded as challenge and accusation, 'You want him to

6

go out there with his shirt open like a bad John for them to knock him down before he even start to live?'

There were times I stood between my parents, my fingers trembling on the top-most button of my shirt, knowing that, with my three-quarter length pants, my cleaned head, and my socks collapsed around my ankles, to button it would be to complete my costume of clown. I look at my father. There is a distant waiting in his eyes. It is as if at any instant his time can come, but that right then is not his time. His ambition is to open a radio repairs shop. That will come when he has completed the Radio Repairs Course he has been taking off and on for as long as I can remember. His real work is a woodcutter. He is an axe man. They have given him the name Bull. He is a strong man, with strong arms and neck and a face unto which in times like these he is always trying to force a smile. He has learnt that the smile is a superior weapon, that it can create ease, give a sense of control; but, it is not a weapon that he has mastered; it is one that masters him; so that far from giving the effect he desires, it twists his face into another truth, the truth. It makes him look weak, appealing, sly, as someone who is telling a lie.

Life has embarrassed him. It is always proving him wrong. 'It is my fault,' he says, triumphantly. He has chosen to be loyal to unprofitable enterprises and to have as friends people who cannot help him, and has allowed currents that he could have floated on to pass him by. All sorts of opportunities have passed him in this way. Sometimes he talks in a wistful voice of the Water Scheme days when so much timber was there to be reaped. And where was he? He was bound on another man's estate, planting orange trees and a mango orchard. The same thing happened when the Americans opened their Base. The Radio Repairs Course, that is what he looks forward to completing now.

'Button up your shirt,' he says, after a long enough pause, finally, as if each time, this time too, he had thought it through and, sadly, saw no alternative but to bend to the weight and sway of the world. 'Button it up!' his voice trying to be firm, in it the mild, the tentative promise of a future time when by some power yet unknown – win a sweepstake maybe, complete the Radio Repairs Course – he will provide us with the freedom to be free.

And my mother, hearing this dream and treason in his voice, but, happy that she had got him to acknowledge the predominance of a power greater than all our efforts, says, almost with sorrow, 'Yes, let him button it up. When he get big, he could be a stickfighter like you and your brother, Bango.'

I look at my father. It occurs to me that he is in some kind of a jam, some trap, some hole, something that has to do with money and stickfighting and jail: that has to do with setting a proper example for the children, with his inviting his friends home to eat, my mother would say, 'as if we own a grocery,' and when the drums beat at Carnival time, his disappearing, with the stickmen lead by his brother Bango, to Sangre Grande and Moruga and Mayaro. My mother saying to him, 'Follow Bango, Bango aint have a child to his name. Follow Bango. Bango have three woman to mind him.'

On the day of Christmas Eve my father usually went and helped Mr Sylvestre butcher a pig, and in the evening he would come home with a few drinks of rum in his head and in his hands a choice piece of pork and a coiled length of black pudding, and after he put down the meat and had a bath and something to eat, he would take up his *cuatro* and his two *shac shacs* and go into the kitchen where my mother would have started seasoning the meat, 'I going down the road to see what the boys doing.' And he would be gone until maybe, sometime, Christmas day when he would come up the front steps with the rest of the *parang* band and stand on the verandah, with his head bent sideways and his eyes closed, singing in his rasping bass voice the plaintive serenades, his fingers flying over the strings of the *cuatro* cradled in his arms, and my mother would throw open the door for him, for them, and, with the rest of the band, he would enter, like a stranger, the drawing room, with its curtains and its polish and its paint, with everything already on the table, the rum and the wine and the ham and the sweetbread and the ginger beer and the sorrell and the cake, the magnificent testament of her servitude, the yearly affirmation of her martyrdom and reproach. He would enter, saying to the men accompanying him, 'Wipe your foot. Wipe your foot! Don't dirty the lady floor.' And he would play music and sing and drink and eat and leave with them, returning home maybe a day or two later, not content simply with making the rounds of the village, but, finding it necessary to go by his sister in Valencia, by his brother-in-law in Sangre Grande or by one of his cousins in Biche. And he would stand before my mother with his cap twisted on his head, his face wrinkled and his eyes twinkling with a guilty and refreshed look, for my mother to say, 'Be glad that you have a woman like me,' turning away from his attempt to embrace her and so make what might have passed for forgiveness its own punishment.

At such times, the lie of his smile would weaken his face, and with his fumbly muscular awkwardness, he would look from my mother to Michael and me; and again I would get this sense of a man mired in some swamp, stuck in some muddy hole in a world that was not the world, this sense of a strength that could not find a way to break through to that world, to that freedom that I was learning we did not yet possess.

'Somebody have to keep it up, Pearl. Somebody have to play the music and go round by people for Christmas and bring some merriment,' he would say.

'And you always have to be the one,' my mother says.

'Somebody have to keep up these things. Somebody,' astonished at her show of indifference.

'You want me to stop?' he asked one day.

'I don't want you to dead,' my mother said.

And he limped away with his wound and his strength, with his *cuatro* like a toy in his fist, to bleed slowly from the wounds of his loyalties and his guilt, to grow quiet with the routine of his woodcutting and the slow magical fiddling with the derelict radios which people had abandoned and brought for him to resurrect, until Carnival came and, as my mother would say, 'the blood fly up in his head,' and he leave again, leave radio and axe and forest and take up his stick and go down to the junction to the stickfights by Loy shop and meet Bango and

9

Mano and John and Ragoo and William and go until Ash Wednesday when he would return home, burdened with repentance.

'Leave him alone, Pearl,' Aunt Irene advises. 'He don't gamble. He don't drink too much rum. And, far as I know, he not friending with no other woman.'

'You see me interfering with him? You see me holding his foot? He is a man do exactly what he want. I don't ask him no question. He go, he come ... ' she said, with a kind of righteous exasperation.

One day we were all in the kicthen, my mother, Aunt Irene, Michael and Ronnie and me. My father wasn't there.

'Me and your father getting married,' my mother said. 'Not anything big. Just a few of us. Just family.' As if she felt that she had been too casual, she added, 'I telling you all this so you will know, not for you to broadcast anything. Is between us, you understand. We not having anything big. Just a few of us in the church. We'll have to get new shoes for the two of you.'

'Kiss your mother,' Aunt Irene said to us. 'Say congratulations.'

Michael kissed her first. Then I went and threw my arms around her neck.

'If is anybody to kiss is their father,' Ma said. 'Is his idea. He's the one who decide after thirteen years living together to do this thing. He believe it will bring him luck, will change him, make him stop galavanting.'

'You can't believe that that is all, Pearl. Love. The man love you. He don't want you to leave him.'

'Leave? Where I leaving to go at this hour of my life?' my mother asks. She turns to us: 'Is for you all,' she said, 'to give you a name now that you getting big in the world. So don't let him down. He have his ways, but, he try. He trying.'

'You not frighten, Pearl?' Aunt Irene asks.

'Sure I frighten,' Ma said, jokingly. 'You know they say when the living good without wedding, the ring does spoil the thing.'

'Let it spoil, Pearl. You is Mistress Jordan now. Mistress Jordan! Let them take that!' Aunt Irene's full-throated, victorious laughter suggesting that the impending marriage was my mother's personal triumph accomplished against the wishes and will of the world.

Ma smiled charitably, 'Darling, I don't worry with people. People could say what they want.'

I was surprised. Seeing me looking at her, she signalled away Michael and me, 'Big people talking now.'

With the wedding coming, a quietness settled upon our household. In it, relatives descended. It was the women who came, the big, majestic women of our family, with their colourful headties and their scents of herbs and incense, with the mysterious air of priestesses who had come to initiate my mother into new rites connected with marriage. Suddenly, they were everywhere, cooking and baking and cleaning. My mother worked among them, allowing herself to be directed by this strong female force, and, for once, she was the woman, bride, fussed over and waited upon.

With relatives among us, and about to enter her new status, she grew calm, gentle. Now she was less strict, her voice was softer and had in it lots of patient laughter. It was a period of grace for Michael and me, and we took advantage of it, figuring that she wouldn't bawl us out in front of these strangers. And she tried to keep up the fiction of softness and gentle persuasion; but, on occasions, she would pull us aside, 'What the hell wrong with you? You don't know how to behave.' But, in front of her sisters or cousins, she would say sweetly, 'Michael and Travey, boys, you not tired hearing me talk?' as if she had all the patience in the world.

My father had brought in a few of his friends from the village to help him build a tent in the yard. The quality of his silence was different too. The house, always a place where my mother reigned, had never been his domain; now, with all these women about, he seemed an intruder. In a way, the presence of outsiders brought him closer to my mother. Suddenly I realised that they had secret signs between them, glances, gestures, lifting of eyebrows, at which signals they would move towards each other to discuss what they felt needed to be discussed. My father had a sense of satisfaction about him. It was as if he accepted to himself that he was doing something noble, something that would make my mother happy. He was overjoyed. It was almost embarrassing seeing him so pleased with himself. When he spoke to her out in the yard, he would linger, holding her hands in his own, or place a hand on her shoulders, making a public declaration of the nobility of his resolve. He expressed this warmth to my brother and me as well, involving us in the work around the house, directing us to sweep the yard or to do any other chore which our skill and size permitted.

Holding the two of us around our shoulders, he would say, 'You, bring the water; you, go and get the coconut branches.' It felt good.

Seeing him in this mood, Uncle Bango, who was helping with the building of the tent, said, 'You shoulda do this thing thirteen years ago.'

'Yes,' Pa said, 'I really waste time. But now all that change. I am a family man now.'

Sometimes, though, listening to him talk about stickfighting and the musicians and the rum drinking, I got to glimpse a new side of him, that side that had always been outside of home, outside with the men. It was this he was trying to give up, this part of his life that had to do with the men, the stickfighting and *parang*. After such bouts of reminiscence, he would say, almost as a joke, 'Well, all that done now. I hope everybody hearing me. After this wedding, don't look for me in the stickfight and *parang*. I is a family man now. Is me and my wife and my children.'

'Pearl, you must help him,' Aunt Irene said. 'These things is his life.'

'And I and his children not his life?' Ma asked.

'You is his life in a different way.'

'Bertie is not a young man again, you know. Bertie is not twenty. Today everybody looking to progress. These things must stop. These friends can't put him nowhere.'

'You know him better than me,' Aunt Irene said. 'Is your husband.'

12

For the wedding day, Aunt Irene left with my mother to go by another aunt where she would dress to go to the church. We were left with my father and another aunt, my father's sister.

'How I look?' Pa asked, when he was ready to leave for the church. 'Too dress up, eh?'

He had bought a new pair of trousers and new shoes, but he had on the same jacket that he used for funerals. He stood with his broad shoulders, big, new-looking, with a rosebud in the lapel of his jacket, and a small handkerchief in his breast pocket.

'Just good,' Aunt Hilda said. 'Today is a day to dress up.'

'I feel too dress up, though. This dressing up business is not for me.' I could see that he was pleased with how he was looking.

We went with them to the church, Michael and me. I saw my mother standing in her white dress, with her bouquet, not looking like my mother at all, but strangely glamorous and bewildered. She had gloves on.

Michael and me were dressed alike, shirt, short pants and a tie; Ronnie wore long pants and a scissors tail jacket, and he wore gloves.

Aunt Irene wore gloves too, pink, like the rest of her outfit. The only other colour was the black lace over her hat.

After the ceremony in the church, we all went home, and it was fete, with a small band of musicians, Ambrose and the Boys. It was supposed to be a small thing; but, in Cunaripo, you didn't have a small fete. People didn't have to be invited. They just came. All about men were in jackets and ties in the hot afternoon and food was sharing and people were eating. We were just churning the second batch of ice cream when Uncle Bango came outside and said, 'Everybody, inside!' The music had stopped and there was to be speech-making. They had invited the Forest Ranger of the district to say a few words as well as Uncle Pascal, who was a guard on the railways. Uncle Bango said that he couldn't let the occasion pass without saying something, got up and made a speech. The Forest Ranger talked. Uncle Pascal talked.

Then it was my father's turn. I watched him standing huge and awkward in his shirt and tie (he had taken off his jacket).

13

'You know I is no speechmaker,' he said. 'Just that I glad that you all come, and everybody having a good time. Only one thing I want everybody to know is that now I married and I intend to live like a married man. Now, let's take a drink to the bride, Mistress Jordan.'

Everybody applauded and then they had the cake sticking, with Aunt Irene singing the song, and then it was back to dancing and I to eating cake and drinking ice cream.

After the wedding, Pa was in the radio repairs room often, and sometimes in the night, doing my home lessons, I would hear the scratching and screeching of the radio and sometimes snatches of Spanish from the radio he was repairing. We had a lot of cake left over from the wedding, after giving to all our relatives. A month after the wedding, we were still eating cake.

Then Christmas was coming, and the *parang* band was beginning to go about the village, serenading people. Pa's *cuatro* remained hanging from a string in the living room near the hat rack. It was strange to hear the music and to know that he wasn't there with them. Nobody didn't talk about it. Then, with a week to go before Christmas day, he left one evening, saying to my mother, 'I just going down the road to carry this *cuatro* for Felix.' It was a Friday evening. Monday morning they brought him home. It was Christmas Eve too.

It was the day after that same Christmas. We were going to church. He wasn't going. He had long since given up going to church; but, he had come out on the verandah to watch us go. Aunt Irene and my mother were still inside finishing dressing, and down in the yard, Ronnie, dressed already in his cowboy suit and with a toy pistol in a holster, one of the gifts from his mother, was drawing his gun and firing at Michael who, more indifferent to Ronnie than I could ever be, stood at the edge of the flower garden oblivious to the shots that were speeding through his body.

I come out of the house and am going to meet Michael and Ronnie. I pause. 'I going, Pa.'

He looks at me. I suppose that he sees that I am growing. I am eleven. Next September I will be twelve.

14

'You going,' he says, and pushes a hand into a side pocket and brings out a coin, the royal sum of six cents. 'Change it,' he says, handing it to me. 'Don't put all in the collection plate.'

'Thanks.' I am watching him. He is beginning to grey. It is really strange to see him at home on Boxing Day. He grins uncomfortably.

'Your mother tell me you doing well at school. That is good. That is very good, eh.'

I nod, yes. In fact, I had passed to go to the Exhibition class, and Ma had made a great fuss over me.

'And in the new year coming here you going to be in Teacher George class. They say he is a serious teacher, eh?'

'Yes, Pa.'

'Good. It good to have a serious teacher. You can't skylark when you have a serious teacher. You can't skylark at all ... Eh?'

I smiled.

'You not going to be like me, you know. No. You not going to be like your father. Last year ... When it was that William son make a place in the Exhibition and went to the college?'

'It wasn't last year.'

'No,' he said, correcting himself. 'Wasn't last year. Was two, three ... Yes, three years. Time. Look at time, eh? But William son wasn't just bright. William son use to study. Sometimes your mother is right,' he said, pushing his hand into his pocket. 'You have to learn to leave people behind you if you want to move on. You have to learn to be alone. You can't carry friends with you. You can't carry people with you. William son study alone.'

While we were talking, we had walked away from the door to the other end of the verandah.

Then they appeared, my mother first, her handbag over one arm, in the same hand, her fan, in the other, her prayerbook. Her hat tilted saucily at an angle, Aunt Irene's doing I was sure, stout, her dress fluffy, fanning herself already; and behind her, Aunt Irene, poised, serene, with the spectacles she sometimes wore as part of her fashion, her slim, thick body

15

rustling, on her face, a flustered assurance in anticipation of the stir she would create, Pa saying, 'Nice! Nice!' bowing his head and smiling. Aunt Irene singing out, 'How you like how your girls looking?'

'Champion,' Pa saying, a bit too gaily, trying to get the attention of my mother who, self-conscious and with her own rustling, descended the steps with an air of grandeur, acting out a rebuke that we did not believe she felt.

I turn to follow them. I look at my father, 'I going, Pa.'

He looks at me. 'Wait.' He makes a step towards me, on his face is a humbled softness now that he no longer sought to struggle with the imitation of a smile. 'Button up your shirt, Travey.' And as I looked at him, 'Yes. Don't frighten, button it up,' nodding encouragement as if, yes, it was all right. It was the thing to be done.

I felt a strange relief and a flow of sadness. It was as if we had come to an end, the two of us. The hoping was done. It was as if he had come finally to acknowledge that he could no longer ask me to wait upon his dreams, that my freedom was to be severed from his own, that I was to go on alone. 'Button up your shirt, man,' gently, firmly, with comradeship and compassion and love, laying a hand on my shoulder, his eyes lighting up with a new wisdom, as if he had just glimpsed the possibility that this burden that he had come to acknowledge that I must bear might be the armour to protect me against that power that he had himself not triumphed over, but had not surrendered to.

TWO

Let me not make a martyr of myself. I begin to button up my shirt. It is an act that becomes for me quite grave, almost holy. I feel myself the bearer of a redemptive penance that shall lead me to glory, that shall remove the strange burden from my father and make my mother proud of me. I am our hope. I shall become a scholar, a saint.

Now, without complaint, I suffer myself to endure Mr Fitzie's shearing, so much that my mother, who had come to

16

expect the ritual of my protest, becomes puzzled; then she gets worried.

There is a sense of largeness about my mother. Not only is she physically large, she moves large, she talks loud, she fusses, she bustles, she flies up. She prowls our world like a setting hen, with its eyes suspicious and its wings fluffed, as if to present a greater mass against the catastrophies she predicts and expects. She is suspicious of too much tenderness. It is a luxury she is not sure we can afford. It is to be disguised, dispensed discreetly. One time I saw her come from cooking to the kitchen window to look at a scene of my father coming in from the garden to the back of the house.

My father is carrying a bundle of grass on his head. He is also bringing in our two goats. With one hand he holds the two ropes binding the goats, the other he uses to steady the grass on his head. The goats tug, each in a different direction. My father strains to hold them, using the one hand. My mother is looking at him. On her face is the woman she had succeeded so well in hiding, caring, wonder, fascination, humour. That woman has been superseded by The Mother, the great pillar and presence anchored in enduring. She turns and sees that I am looking at her. 'Boy!' she cries, suddenly flustered, as if she had been caught in an act of subversion, as if she had revealed to me too much of that other person that is also herself, 'What you stand up there looking up in my face for? Go and help him!'

Oh, Mother! I want to cry out. I want to run and hug her. She allows herself a smile, shooing me away.

When she worries, it is with the hen's boisterous camouflage, as if fussiness and bustle will turn back the problem. I read of mothers who pick up their children and kiss their hurt. Aunt Irene acts like that with Ronnie: 'Come, sweetheart. What wrong with my baby?' My mother looks on in amusement, believing that Aunt Irene is performing something she has seen acted on the screen of, maybe, the De Luxe cinema.

My mother says, 'Come on. Get up,' as if tenderness, when we fall, must not be allowed to get in the way of our rising again.

After she had puzzled and wondered about me long enough, she confronts me, large, Amazonian, 'What happen to you?'

17

And already I am trembling, for in our household illness is also an extravagance. 'What you mean, Ma?'

'You very well know what I mean. You about the house poorly poorly; you sitting down quiet and getting your hair trim; you buttoning up your shirt without nobody telling you nothing. You very well know what I mean. You sick? Somebody cuff you in your belly? You get a fall? You was in a fight?' All while she is firing her questions, she is pressing the back of her hand against my cheek, on the skin of my neck, checking my temperature. She peers into my eyes. Her frown deepens. 'Take off your shirt!'

'Ma?'

'Take off your shirt!'

I take off my shirt. She thumps my chest with the back of a crooked index finger, sounding me.

'Ma, nothing aint happen to me.'

She questions my brother in the same aggressive style, 'Michael, what it is happen to Travey? He was in a fight? He get a fall?'

Michael is a born suspect. He stammers, he fumbles, he looks around furtively. It appears to her that he is hiding something. Michael, however, doesn't know yet of my conversion, my sainthood.

'He get a fall? Michael, did your brother get a fall?'

Baffled, she circles. Later she returns to me, 'You have worms!' she announces, with an incontestible certainty, a little bit amazed that the diagnosis could have escaped her. 'Purge!' with a kind of glee, the one prescriptive word, remedy and punishment.

'But, Pearl?' And now it is Aunt Irene's turn to be amused. 'Pearl, what it is you want this boy to do? You cut his hair like a Nazi and you get vex when he complain; he stop complaining, and now you find he acting strange. What you really want him to do?'

Quickly, before she can hide it, a smile flashes across my mother's face, and, for a moment she seems constrained to give an explanation, but, she doesn't. 'Purge!' she repeats, insistently, hurrying away, trying to contain the smile and return the severity to her look.

But, I had seen her smile. It puzzles me. This same mother, who forces me to have my head trimmed clean and my shirt buttoned up, is the mother who wants me to struggle against having these things done to me. Oh, mother!

Purged, buttoned up, greased down and tame, I go to school with the quiet pathos of a clown, in the masquerade that undermines my natural male aura. I am bullied by the boys, dismissed by the girls. They sense my meekness. They give me the nickname, 'Mice', in reference to my fine, protruding teeth. On those days when my haircut is fresh, the boys surround me, pull my cap down over my eyes and rain clouts on my head. I am confused. I wonder if I should fight back. Do saints fight back?

To my brother Michael, my distress is all a joke. He laughs when the boys clout me. Sometimes at home he teases me and, in a mood of mischief, he tells Ronnie what the boys at school do to me. Now Ronnie begins to call me 'Mice'. Now Ronnie wants to clout me.

'Ronnie!' I warn. 'Ronnie!' But, Ronnie is not easily put off. He persists. He believes that among us, he has a special licence. 'Ronnie!'

Even my mother grows impatient with me, 'Sit down there and bawl, "Ronnie! Ronnie!"' she shouts, tired of my whining.

Michael, the traitor, laughs; and Ronnie makes a funny face at me. It is Michael's behaviour that most pains me.

Michael is fourteen. He has already lost his chance at a college exhibition. Now he must study to get his School Leaving Certificate. In another year he will leave school, 'To dig dirt,' my mother says, 'Or to pick coconut on the white people estate ... You will be an A-one coconut picker,' she tells him. 'Don't learn your lessons. Follow Alexis' son and the other nowherian one they calling Scull. Follow them. You will have good dirt digging companions.'

Michael is unworried. He protests nothing. He sits down in perfect peace while Mr Fitzie trims him. The cleaner the trim, the more is Michael delighted. If there are zugs on his head, he wears them as medals. Nobody needs to tell Michael to button up his shirt. Michael buttons every button right up to his neck.

'You look like you from the orphanage,' my mother tells him, trying to shame him. 'Like you have no owner.' Michael grins. He doesn't have in his possession a school shirt which is not stained with cashew juice or mango sap, nor one with a complete set of buttons. Michael buttons up his shirt with pins. With his impassive face and occasional wry grin, he goes to school with the solemn air of a triumphant clown, in a parody of the neatness which my mother and the school seek to impose upon him. At school, 'Priest' is the nickname they have given him. He spends his time with a gang of boys even more worthless than himself. Their nicknames are self-explanatory: Scull, Belly, Police. They steal children's lunches; they raid mangoes from the estate; they leave school to go fishing and smoke cigarettes; and once the principal promised to expel them when he caught them underneath the school house peering into a mirror they had placed underneath a hole in the flooring, above which one of the Standard Five girls was sitting. They were tough.

As Michael's brother, I had been somewhat exempted from the terrors of their attention; but, now, with my sainthood, they feel no restraint. I had changed. As a candidate for the college exhibition, I suspect that I had begun to draw myself away from them. I was becoming the scholar, the hope. I was becoming tame. Now, on the playing field and at the pipe where we drink water, they jostle me. They are out for me, I think.

Earlier the clouts I received from them when I went to school with a freshly trimmed head were simply ritual, something that made me feel part of the school, part of the boys, part of a brotherhood. There was never anything vicious about them. Now, thanks to Scull and company, these clouts begin to sting. I began to feel humiliated, abused. At first I accepted them as part of the price I had to pay for my escape, my sainthood. They wouldn't go on forever. Soon, I would pass my examination and leave them and the school. I tried to buoy myself up with thoughts of my ascension, my coming glory; but, having to face these fellows every third Monday morning, in meekness, I felt something surrendering in myself, a pride, a spirit, a self. I began to feel myself getting away from me. I realised that I had to pay attention to the presentness of my world or forever surrender. I thought of my father and the promise that I had made that morning. I went to Michael.

'Michael, tell Scull and them that I don't want them to clout me.'

To Michael, that is not possible. As far as he is concerned, it is a rule. 'They clout everybody,' he says. 'They clout me too. They can't change the rules for you.'

'Is not the same, Michael. You is their friend. They want to hurt me.'

Michael cannot understand what I am saying. He doesn't want to. We quarrel.

'Just tell them I don't want any one of them touching my head. Rule or no rule. I not playing. I don't clout nobody and I don't want nobody to clout me.'

I do not know if Michael told them how I felt. For my part, I tried to keep out of their way. I cannot escape them; they are everywhere. In all of it, Michael is an onlooker. I am alone. One Monday morning I go to school with a freshly trimmed head, courtesy of Mr Fitzie. The band of fellows is in the schoolyard waiting for me. In front is Scull, next to him stand Police and Belly. Michael is with them. I am wearing a cap.

'You have a nice trim,' Scull says, grinning.

Scull is long, bony and tough. He is, what is called, double-jointed, a condition which denotes abnormal strength. He is the wicketkeeper for the school's cricket team. At football, he is the goal keeper. He makes flips and walks on his hands. His bleary eyes and frightening grin have earned him his nickname.

I say nothing.

'We mustn't touch his head. His head is too precious,' Belly says, mocking me, at the same time edging closer.

'No, we mustn't touch his head,' Scull says; and with one deft movement of his long bony hand, makes a snatch at my cap. Only after I had ducked, did I realise that he hadn't meant seriously to remove the cap. For the moment, he was just playing with me.

'A very nice trim,' said Belly, also making a snatch at my cap. The boys had closed in. I was surrounded.

Making fun of me, Police clapped his hands and at the same instant reached out to touch my head. Seeing him in the motion, I started to swing, and, to his surprise and mine, my fist sank into the firm flesh of his belly. As he stepped back to move in more seriously, the school bell rang.

'Friday,' gasped Police, as we made for the lines.

Friday is the day for fighting. Being the last day of school for the week, it is the safest day to get your clothes dirty; and, being two days before the start of the new week, it allows the possibility that the news would not get to the school master, and if it did there would be two days for him either to forget or for it to seem distant on the following Monday.

'You crazy or what?' Michael said to me, when we were home that evening. 'You going to fight Police? Police will kill you. Don't expect me to come in, you know.'

Of the gang, Police is the most dangerous because he is the one with the least sense of humour. He will be the most unforgiving. Scull is their leader, Belly is a comic. He is nothing himself, but gets his status from being with the other. He is their caddy boy. Police doesn't laugh. He is fourteen, like Michael. He has an inner vexation and viciousness. He is a bully. He wears his step-father's cut down blue serge trousers which still carry the wide loops made especially for the thick police belt. On his arms are outlined belt marks, stripes, where the lashes from his step-father's floggings have left their mark.

'Say sorry. Go and tell him you sorry,' Michael says.

'Say sorry? I can't go and tell the man I sorry.'

'Give him something, then. You have a pan of marbles. Give them to him.'

'You feel he will take it?'

'I will talk to him,' Michael said.

Next day Michael came to tell me that it was okay. I could give Police the pan of marbles and all would be forgiven. The pan of marbles was a Christmas present from Aunt Irene. I had kept them safely because I hardly used them. I didn't like to play marbles. The fact is, I wasn't good at it. Sometimes I played with Ronnie, who was the only one around who was a worse player than me; but, we always ended up quarrelling. I didn't need the marbles.

I put the marbles in by book bag next day and went to school. I saw Police, but, I didn't give them to him.

'Why you didn't give him the marbles?' Michael asked.

I didn't even know why. Really, I didn't know. I had intended to give them to him. 'Tomorrow,' I said. 'I will give them tomorrow.'

Michael is dissatisfied. He had already told the fellows of my forthcoming peace offering. Now I was making him look like a fool. 'What you waiting for?' he asks. 'You want to fight him? I not going to come in, you know.'

'You want to give them to him for me?'

'No,' says Michael. 'He want them from you.'

For three days of that week I took the marbles to school with me. Thursday evening I still had them. Somehow I had not been able to bring myself to give them over.

'Tomorrow is Friday,' Michael said. 'That is all I have to say.'

On a Thursday evening in Cunaripo, the stores are closed and the rum shops shut. This evening Main street is quiet and looks wide and the sun is bright. Charcoal burners, on their way to the forest and their charcoal pits, sit on a bench in front of Kee's rum shop, drinking and making merry, singing old love songs and ancient calypsos. Mano, my uncle, is playing his *cuatro*, accompanying them. With them is Priscilla, the only woman there, dancing by herself, her shoulders bent in a tender crouch, her arms wrapped around her body and her eyes closed with the sweetness of memories.

'Good evening, Miss Priscilla,' I say.

'Good evening, lover,' she answers, opening reddened eyes that sparkle with sorrow, winking at me, closing them again.

When Priscilla was young, my mother says, it didn't have anybody in Cunaripo who could dress like her, and nobody so good looking. When it had a dance fellars used to line up just to dance with her, she was so popular. People see a drunkard now, my mother says. But, in those days, Priscilla was a star. Then she went to the city. She went Venezuela. Her pictures used to be in the papers. She was a model. She used to give away dresses to her relatives. Good good dresses, she used to give away; pretty pretty dresses. A big shot man was engaged to marry her. She had a good job in the civil service. She was up in society. But, poor Priscilla see what she shouldn't see; she hear what she shouldn't hear. Her boss was a big racketeer, defrauding the country of thousands and thousands of dollars. He bribe everybody, but not Priscilla. She give evidence against him in the enquiry. That was the end of her. She lose her job. The man that she was to marry leave her. Her family who she used to give those pretty dresses to disown her. They try to poison her. She come back to Cunaripo to try to catch herself. They drag her down. They drag her down. She start to drink rum. She lose her looks, her reputation. People forget her, my mother says; but, not my mother. Aunt Irene remembers her too. They talk of her. They remember when she was a star. She, my mother, demands that, no matter what, we be respectful to Priscilla. Whenever I see her, I say 'Good evening, Priscilla'; and she says, 'Good evening, lover'. I am a little scared of her.

In front the rum shop now, the scene, that a while ago was so merry, turns ugly. Priscilla's performance had taken her to where the men have their bottle of rum. She attempts to take a drink. One of the men protests.

'Get away from here, you dirty woman. Go and bathe before you touch that rum.'

'You talking to me?' Priscilla puts on a baby voice and rolls her eyes flirtatiously. She thinks she knows how to break their hearts.

'You, yes,' the man shouts. 'Go and bathe before you touch this rum.'

'You talking to me? He talking to me?' Priscilla, looking around, now the centre of attention. With the coquetry of a strip tease, she lifts her dress and shows her petticoat. Swinging her hips, fluttering her eyelids, she cries, 'Who is dirty? Look! Look!' lifting her dress higher.

Provoked further, for there are those who egg her on,' Show more! Show more! Show everything!' she lifts her petticoat and

24

reveals her undergarment and her scrawny legs. 'You see it? You see how clean?' She advance upon the man who had made the remark, gyrating her hips, 'Come on, show your drawers. Show them. I show you mine, now, show yours. See whose is dirty.'

'Show it, Johnny!' the other men chant. 'Don't make her make you shame.'

Johnny begins to laugh, an embarrassed laughter. His laughter is his surrender, 'Come, Priscilla, come,' he invites her. 'Come and take a drink. Go on children, go on.'

I walk away, leaving behind me their laughter. There at the roundabout is Corporal, barebacked, wearing his own home-made baton at his waist, standing in the middle of the road, directing traffic. On his head is a chamber pot, his helmet; his leggings are a tangle of dried banana leaves wrapped around his feet, from ankles to his knees. He is barefooted.

Earlier, I had passed Mussolini on a bench. He is an old stickfighter who keeps vigil at that corner, with a stick in his hand. He wears a battered, black jacket, its pockets stuffed with stones, for he is at war with the schoolchildren who tease him about a sore that is rotting away one of his feet. Some of us run when we see him, others stand a safe distance away and taunt him, and run when he gets up to give chase.

When I get to Federation Cafe, I will see Science Man, who my father says, 'book send mad', who, during the war, they say, was sentenced to a term in prison for making a radio. Now Science Man prowls the street with a grimace on his face and now and again butts his head forcefully against the wood of the telephone post. Britain, in her unchanged dress of red, white and blue; Graham, with his hernia, Pretty Foot, our transvestite; Fowl, who still crows like the cock he stole from Mother Alice; the Shango priestess. These are our celebrities. Their escapades, their fights, their moments of madness, their sayings, these are the subjects of our conversations. And about each of them is a story: pride that has fallen; ambition that overleaped itself. Each story ends victoriously in defeat, penance, apology. This was our folklore. Until that Thursday evening, I had not put them all together in that way. It was then that I felt the weight of their

25

apology and defeat for the first time; and, for the first time, I looked at our town.

The architects of Cunaripo have placed the police station on a hill commanding the main street. On another hill, the steeple of the Roman Catholic church rises against the sky like a shaft of white light; seeing it, men make the sign of the Cross, women genuflect. Men, coming out of Kee's rum shop, stumble upon the serene and anchored power of the police station, with its thick masonry and its Union Jack and its walk of whitewashed flagstones, about it a distant and secret air, like that of a monastery; and they make a bow, not a bow of bending the back, but one of straightening the knees, recognising before them a power than can render them as sober as the surrounding estate's cocoa trees, standing in their green and lavish silence, offering pods that are crimson breasts, golden eyes; while behind these, below the bulging muscles of the mountain's back, the suspenseful forest watches through the window panes of white eyes. Overpowered by the sense of penance and apology, I head for home.

I must escape. Tomorrow, for sure, I will make Police a gift of my marbles and I would be done with them, with this. I was thinking how wonderful it would be to win a college exhibition and leave and go to college and get away from this place.

I must have bent my head just then to blink away the water that filled my eyes. When I lifted it again, there, through the glaze of tears, I see coming towards me, this giant, dancing in a tall loose-jointed ease, his shirt collar turned up, his chest unbuttoned, his hat at a tilt and the sunshine glinting off his face. It was my uncle, Bango. He was whistling. I felt a sudden thrill. I stopped and gazed at him. He waved a hand and winked in salute in recognition, 'Bull!' he exclaimed, calling me by my father's nickname; and, still in his beat, in tune with his rhythm, he went on. Bull, he had called me. In that call was comradeship, acknowledgement, was a pride in me, in himself, in all our family. I felt a sense of thankfulness, I felt saved. Out of this landscape, I had plucked a hero.

I would like to embellish Uncle Bango with power and purpose and a war, give him two pistols and a rifle and a double bandolier;

and, with a *sombrero* tied around his neck and falling on his shoulders, put him on a white horse and make him a bandit chieftain at the head of forty, fifty, a hundred lean desperadoes who appear out of nowhere to battle for the poor. I would like to tell of his being pursued by the cavalry, riding through a hail of bullets to meet the woman that is waiting for him, and his name will be Pancho or Fidel or Che. But that would obscure the truth of this story. I am not blinded by Uncle Bango.

I know he was a hero of a world shrunken to the size of a village street or gambling club or stickfight ring, that his name was linked with streetfighting and gambling, that beyond the limits of Cunaripo hardly anyone would know him. We talked about him at home. He worked irregularly. My mother says he had three women minding him. Pa knows him as a wood worker. He could dance bongo, fight stick and he sculptured heads from dried coconuts. But, he was all I had to pit against the desolate humbling of our landscape. What did he bring?

I suppose I must call it style. It was not style as adornment, but style as substance. His style was not something that he had acquired to enhance an ability; rather, it existed prior to any ability or accomplishment – it was affirmation and self looking for a skill to wed it to, to save it and maintain it, to express it; it was self searching for substance, for meaning. He sometimes wore white, buff shoes. They were always spotless. One night at a fete, Cut Cake, a petty thief, stepped on his shoes and refused to say sorry. When he admonished him, Cut Cake drew a knife. The story, which circulated through the village afterwards, and which came to us at school, was that Uncle Bango paused. And before he butt Cut Cake, he said, 'Don't do that stuff, kid.' No doubt it was something that he had heard in a movie; but, the spirit, the desire for meaning, the style, that was Uncle Bango's.

That evening, though, his one word, salutation, greeting, 'Bull!' conveyed that he was proud of me, that I was part of the struggle, that he was depending on me to achieve with my education the substance that he had been seeking all his life. In a way, I was a hero to him too, to his whole generation. For them, heroism had never meant the surrender of the self.

Next day, as soon as I step out of range of our house, I turn up my shirt collar, undo the topmost button of my shirt, give my khaki pants an added fold, my costume of clown had been transformed to that of warrior, I became, 'Young Bull', nephew of Bango the stickfighter.

'What you doing?' Michael asked in consternation when he saw me making these adjustments to my person. 'Where the marbles?'

'I don't have them. They home.'

'You don't have them? I serious, you know. If you fighting Police, I not putting a hand.'

'Suit yourself,' I said. At last I was feeling that my life was my own, that somehow I had found a way to confront the penance and apology of our town. I had had a brief conversion; I knew I was saying goodbye to my ambition to be other than my father's son.

That Friday evening as school was out for the day, for the week, two heroes, borne along by the press of their supporters, head for the little clearing behind the playing field on the edge of the forest. I am one of them. Michael is nowhere in sight. I have no idea of tactics, all I know is that I am going to fight Police.

Somebody held my book bag, someone holds my cap. The noise dies down and I square off before Police. Out of the corner of my eyes, I get a look of Michael's face, with a grin on it. What am I really doing here, I am asking myself when I feel myself pushed forward and I find that I am surprised when Police hits me, but I feel a sense of relief at being able to withstand his blow. I strike out. The fight is on. All that I am trying to do is to control my trembling. I am glad when we clinch. Then we are on the ground and I am squirming and squirming to get out of his grasp; and then, by some miracle, I find that I have his neck in the crook of my arm. I press and I squeeze and I hold on for dear life, not because I want to hurt him, but, because I know that if I let go, I am dead. After an eternity, I hear myself scream. Police had clamped his teeth onto my arm. Police had bitten me. The bigger boys part us and we get up. Confusion. Some are inspecting my bitten arm, some are restraining Police roughly.

In keeping with my role as a combatant, I rush to the attack once more, but they hold me back. The fight is over. All around there are outraged voices, 'You bite him! You bite him!' It is a transgression of the rules.

'But, he was choking me,' Police shouts. They don't want to hear him. His supporters feel let down.

'A big man like you,' Scull was saying disdainfully. 'You is a girl or what?'

'I tell you he was choking me,' Police appealed.

I had won the fight on the technicality of the bite.

Suddenly, Michael materialises, 'Look at your clothes!'. In rolling on the ground my clothes had become all dirty, my elbows were bruised as were my knees, and Police's teeth marks were printed on my forearm.

'It bad?' I asked Michael, thinking about my clothes.

'Ma going to soak your tail,' he said.

I dusted myself as best I could, retrieved my belongings and in the middle of a press of supporters, I made for home.

Ma is at the gate waiting for me. My supporters melt . The crook, Michael, had reached home ahead of me and has, no doubt, given her the story.

'Pass in,' she instructs. I go into the house and she follows me. I put down my bag, take off my cap. Arms akimbo, she surveys me. 'Travey, I send you to school to do what?'

I do not answer.

'You don't know what I send you to school for?'

If to such an absurd question I give no answer, it is insolence; if I do answer, I lead myself into the trap she is setting, 'Ma, he hit me first,' I say.

'I am not talking about hitting. I talking about school. I send you to school to do what?'

'But, if he hit me first? Ma, if somebody hit you? If somebody want to clout you?'

'What I send you to school for?'

'To learn, Ma.'

'Yes, to learn. Not to be a fighter; not to be Joe Louis. If somebody hit you, you know what to do. You don't know what to do?'

'Ma, I was outside. I couldn't tell the teacher.'

'Ah, so you know you must tell the teacher if somebody hit you?'

'Yes, Ma.'

'And where Michael was?'

'Michael was there.'

'Michael!' she calls. 'Michael!' My brother appears in his doleful costume of priest. 'Michael, where you was? You mean you stand up there and let them beat your brother?'

Michael starts to give his version of the story. It is jerky and meandering. He tells of his suggestion that I make peace. He tells of his attempts at reconciliation between Police and me.

'So you decide to fight?' Ma asks.

'Ma, I couldn't give him the marbles.'

'And you couldn't tell the teacher either.'

'I beg him to give the marbles to Police. If he did give him the marbles nothing would of happen,' Michael says.

'And because he didn't give the marbles, you stand up and watch them beat him. What kind of brother you is? What happen to the two of you?'

'Nobody aint beat him, Ma. He was winning. He had Police neck locked, and to get away Police had to bite him.'

'Bite? Let me see the bite.'

I show her the teeth marks on my arm. She orders Michael to get the iodine.

'So you is a fighter now,' she says, not without tenderness, holding my arm while I close my eyes and brace myself for the sting of the iodine. 'As for you, Michael, I will speak to your father about you.'

I closed my eyes tightly as the iodine stung. I thought of my father, I felt that I had let him down. The burden that I had agreed to carry, I had rather hurriedly put down. It had seemed so simple then.

'Keep this hand out of water,' she said, daubing the iodine on my elbows now.

'Yes, Ma.'

'It's these games you boys play. This haircut is the whole cause.'

I was glad that I had escaped a flogging. I was ready to rush off.

'And those clothes,' she said sternly. 'You will please wash them yourself.'

'Yes, Ma,' happy that this was to be the price of my reprieve.

'And that head. You better get one of your friends to cut your hair. Fitzie does trim too clean.'

'Yes, Ma. Thank you, Ma.' I wanted to hug her. It was in my eyes.

'Boy,' she said looking down at me. 'What wrong with you now?'

I wanted to hug her, to say, 'I love you'.

'Nothing,' I smiled. With us love had always been expressed in language more tender and tough than words.

THE FIRE EATER'S JOURNEY

That time in Cunaripo everybody was young, and life was sitting with the fellars on the railing at Cunaripo Junction on pay-day Friday and, amid the bedlam of blaring calypsos and cinema announcements and shopping bargains hailed over loudspeakers, and Indian songs blasted from roadside snackettes, watch the thick-fleshed district girls glide with slim briskness between the stalls of the bazaar which wayside vendors made of the stretch of pavement along the shopping area on Main Street, with cots stretched out and the sides of uncovered vans let down to display the clothing and the baskets and the pottery and the cheap wares which they travelled across the island to sell in rural towns on the day when workers got their pay. Life was football, and on a Sunday evening, trotting out with the fellars from underneath the shadow of a breadfruit tree down the hill from the half-built pavilion, into the sunlight of the recreation ground, in the blue jerseys of Penetrators Football Club, when the game was against Cross Winds of Mayaro or Ebonites from Biche, with the referee going to centre the ball and the fellars stretching and prancing and leaping tall, and everybody ready, the ground full, and the girls clustered like bouquets of variegated croton between the clumps of vertivier grass sprouting from the terraced hillside, with the half Chinese gambler who everybody called Japan, coming down the hill, one hand keeping up his trousers and the other uplifting a fistful of bills, shouting, 'Who against Penetrators? Who against Penetrators?' And Big John and Sylvan, two huge Mayaro fishermen, barefooted and in short pants, standing up and bringing money from their pockets and calling, 'Over here! Over here is Cross Winds!' And to hear the silence at a Cross Winds raid and to hear the girls' screams tingling the blood when Berris got the ball and Penetrators swept forward in an invasion, with Kelly and Kenny and Mervyn and Phonso and Blues, and everybody calling, everybody screaming, 'Berris! Berris!' as Berris moved and darted and danced and spun, and Big John's huge hoarse voice thundered, 'Oh Lord, Mayaro. Hold that man!'

Life was Bazaar Day, with the Roman Catholic school hung with palm leaves and old man's beard and frilly paper and balloons, and Joey Lewis band getting ready to play, the musicians picking up their instruments with a torturous slowness, and fellars, thirsty to dance, standing around in a deceptive nonchalance, not even looking at the girls who didn't get to go nowhere except to church and school except on this one day when the church who was organising the Bazaar said it was okay, each man alert for the split-second bang of the piano to launch himself across the room to where the girls sit stewing in the perfumed heat of long-sleeved dresses and can-cans, each man's heart beating with the hope that he would get there on time to be the first to stretch out his hand to that girl that he dying whole day to dance with, and same time hoping that the tune would be a bolero or one of those calypsos with plenty of bounce in it, with space within the music to bring her in and sway with her and hold her gentle and let her go and spin her and make her smile and look up into his face so he could ask her name and tell her his and in that way lay claim to the next dance, and, if she was game, the next. And the next time she passed on Main Street, he would disentangle himself from the conversation on the railing and go to her and if it was all right, if she would smile, he would walk a little way with her, talking to her, the both of them bursting with fright and delight, the two of them too shy to look at the other's face, and in that kind of a magical way she would be his girl.

33

That was the life. The future? The future was a secret that none of the fellars talked about. When police constables were being recruited, those of them who met the height requirement would make the annual pilgrimage to the recruitment centre to see if they would pass the physical and qualify to do the written test. In the evening, still wearing their best clothes, they would return to the railing and talk about the words they had misspelt and the meanings they had missed. I was their authority. Blues stood aside and listened. He wasn't in that because, for all his bulging chest and military bearing, even if he could have mastered the general knowledge and spelling, he was too short for the Police Force to accept him.

Like most of the fellars, Blues had not gone beyond primary school, had learnt no trade; though, if you asked him what trade he knew, he would tell you he was a painter. A couple years earlier, Oliver, a small contractor, had a job to paint some government buildings in the district, and, wanting to do it as cheaply as possible, had taken Blues on. It was his longest period of employment. He called himself a painter after that. And though there was little work in that area, it was a nice thing to say, it sort of located him. For employment, he would get a fortnight's work with the County Council on the road gang, around Christmas or just before Carnival, and once or twice I passed on my motorcycle and saw him waving a branch of green bush, directing traffic away from the area of road his gang was patching. In general though, he picked up a few days with Berisford, mixing cement and sand to make a concrete foundation, or he would go and work for that scamp, Oliver, and have to run all over the place behind him to get the little money he was promised as pay, or he would go out with Poser, who doubled as a truck loader and cinema checker for the owners of Empress cinema, to give out handbills and stick up posters for the coming attractions. But whatever the task, he would come back in time to play football or to sit with the fellars on the railing at the Junction with his bulging chest, square jaw and uncertain grin that gave to his rough sculptured face a look of undeserved wisdom.

Once in a moment of idleness, he had followed Poser and slicked his hair, replacing the soft woolly fluff of it with a greasy messy mop that made him look a little like one of the Katzenjammer Kids, only black. He had used too much dye in the hair preparation and this had caused his hair to begin turning red. Later, with the same rashness, he had shaved off all his hair. He began to wear shirts with the sleeves torn off at the shoulders. With his bulging chest, he looked like a strong-man. It made us laugh. When his hair began to grow back, he started to groom it carefully, and now, he came among us there on the railing, with an almost comical neatness. His long-sleeved shirt was tucked into his trousers and his trousers were pulled up as far above his navel as the length of its crotch would allow, the waist coming to rest way up the rib-cage of his chest; and that chest, whose magnificence impressed even him, was thrown out as he swaggered with a splendid and grotesque elegance that made a boulevard of the ordinary Main Street of Cunaripo. His wasn't the strong tough walk of a desperado of the movies: not the toughness of a Bogart nor the brash brawling imperious ease of a John Wayne, but something more genteel, each step stiff, measured, strong, weighty as a weightlifter's but not as slow, purposeful yet unhurried, the way he would imagine it performed by someone more respectable.

Whenever someone gave him a cigarette, he smoked it with a studied, severe frown, holding it stiffly between index and middle fingers, placing it carefully between lips he had fixed to receive it, drawing in smoke in long, smooth pulls, blowing smoke out in great big puffs, shyly uplifting his eyelids that in inhaling he had closed down, as if he wanted to see who among us was attentive to his performance.

Fellars laughed at his antics; but I saw in them something more subversive.

'Give him a chance, Santo,' Phonso said to me. 'Don't condemn him just so. Listen to him. He have good ideas.'

I couldn't believe that Phonso could be so taken in by Blues. I had listened hard to Blues. He spoke with a lot of superior smiling, in a self-important, put-on tone, his words barely intelligible, his talk weighed down with words he could not pronounce and phrases he did not understand. I could see that he was simply repeating what he had heard from sources he thought to be authoritative in order that the fellars would think him learned. The nonsense he was parroting wasn't even his own. His earlier performances had amused me; but he was over-doing it now. It vexed me that he should think it necessary to go through this kind of mimicry in order to impress fellars who would have accepted him anyway.

One night, I went to the Muslim school to see an acrobatic show put on by Boy Boy and Toy, two self-taught acrobats fron Cunaripo. They had billed it as 'The Greatest Show on Earth'. They did some tumbles and flips, and the big event of the night was the high wire act in which Toy, balancing himself with a long pole, and with Boy shadowing him on the floor below to catch him if he should fall, walked across a length of wire stretched across the ceiling of the school. To give variety, they had three limbo dancers and a contortionist who hopped around on his hands, with his feet twined around his neck and shoulders. There was one other performer. He did two acts. His first was eating fire. He poured some gasolene into his mouth, put a lighted match to it and blew out a stream of flame. For his second act he came on stage wearing only bathing trunks and carrying a huge rice bag filled with broken bottles. The drums began to play as he emptied the contents of the bag onto the stage and smashed the bottle into smaller bits. The tempo of the drums quickened, and when the drumming reached a crescendo, he dashed himself onto the bed of broken bottle. As the drums continued their frenzied beat, he pranced and swam and rolled upon that bed of broken bottle. When the drums ceased, he stepped out without a scratch on his body. This last performer, the Fire Eater and Bottle Dancer, was, I could not believe it, Blues.

I was almost respectful when next I saw him, 'Man, I didn't know you could do such things,' I said. I was really stunned.

'You liked the show?' He was grinning from ear to ear, delighted that he had managed finally to impress me.

'Really, I didn't know that you were so ... good.'

He brushed aside my attempts at praise with an easy magnanimity, 'Toy great, eh?' he said, glowing. 'One of the best in the nation. And everything he learn, he learn right here. Right now we have to put on a little more polish, do a few more show, then we going on a tour. Toy working on it. Port of Spain first, then England.'

'Great,' I said. And, yes, the show was okay. It was all right. It was pretty good, especially for a remote town like Cunaripo. Port of Spain might find it interesting; but, England? I wasn't so sure about England. But now I understood Blues better. I felt relieved. I knew where he was coming from. And when he came on the railings with his antics now, I found myself smiling. We even became sorta friends.

Over the next two years, my last in Cunaripo, they held more shows and I went to all of them. They brought in a fellow who could husk a dry coconut with his teeth. They brought in Baboolal, the magician, who brought a lot of laughter, making people lay green eggs and pee coca-cola. They brought back the contortionist, Rubber Man. After each show, Blues would tell me confidentially, 'We going on tour next month. Getting the contract fixed up. Port of Spain first, then England.' I listened to him. What could I say?

One day he said to me, 'Boy, these local people is hell. They want the show in England, but down here it have so much red tape tying up everything.'

'Yeah,' I said.

Not long after that, I left Cunaripo to go to work in Port of Spain. The red tape tying up Blues' tour had not been unravelled. I left Blues there.

TWO

I am in Port of Spain now. I am going along Independence Square one day when there, coming towards me, through the crowd, not swept along by its bustle, but at his own independent gait, with the same purposeful, self-admiring walk whose elegance had seemed so extravagant in Cunaripo, was Blues. His

37

long sleeves were buttoned at the wrist. He held a folded newspaper in one hand and a cigarette stiffly between fingers of the other. Our eyes met. Immediately my steps quickened. He too seemed to jump at sight of me; but only for a moment. As if he decided that to hurry would undermine the picture of sophistication he was projecting, he restrained himself and, taking a long pull on his cigarette, he strolled towards me.

I felt humbled, rebuked, elated. It all flashed home to me. Blues had not been trying to impress us at all. Blues had been practising for this, preparing for the city. His grand gestures that had so chagrined me were not for Cunaripo; they were for Port of Spain.

He was standing before me now, with a restrained smile that gave an almost forgiving look to his face, holding himself as if on display, with the knowledge that he had turned the tables on me.

'Blues!' I stood paralysed, in a kind of awe before him, and it was he who stretched out a hand for me to shake.

'So what you doing in the city, Santo?' he said, talking with that stilted affectation of superiority. 'I hear you leave Forestry. You in journalism or something? Writing a lot of stories. I see your name in the papers. That's good. You was always a man with ambition. Always had brains. That's why I used to stick close to you. You was the only man in Cunaripo could understand what I say.'

Even with his affectation, I had to admire Blues. I smiled, 'Yes. I'm at *The Standard*. And you?'

'I'm down here with The Show, with Boy Boy and Toy.' He was speaking a bit haltingly, the better to maintain control of the new rhythm of English he was attempting. 'Playing at Paloma night club. They have us book down there. You don't see it in the papers? We have acrobats, calypsonians – Lord Christo, composer. Blakie does come in sometimes. Dancers: Madame Temptation, Rosetta Seduction. Strip tease, you know. It's a great show. The tour ... ' Almost as if he had read my mind, ' ... the tour frustrating everybody. The people in England want the show; but it have all this red tape to go through down here. Papers to fix, arrangements to make. Boy, when I tell you these local people slow.' He had added an impressive raising of his eyebrows to his repertoire of gestures.

I didn't know how to begin to talk to him. I felt myself a traitor. I couldn't understand it. How could I not have seen that Blues had ambition beyond Cunaripo? It was hard to accept; but I had to accept it: I didn't know Blues at all. I had totally underestimated Blues.

He was still displaying himself. 'Let's go and have a beer,' he said. 'Inn and Out,' announcing the name of the place with a sense of familiarity that was supposed to impress me. 'It's up Frederick Street.'

Blues had been in Port of Spain a few months already; but, as we moved up the street, I could sense from him a genuine delight at being at last part of the people, part of the centre of things, there among the shoppers and the newspaper hawkers and coconut vendors standing with feet apart like ancient charioteers hacking off the tops of green coconuts on coconut carts. With his chest thrust out, he strolled with an overpowering grandeur as if he were an honoured guest at a festival with dancing, turning his head self-consciously now and again to see who was admiring him. Now and again he stopped to look in on a display window at the banlon jerseys and tweed jackets displayed on the torso of mannequins with pink faces and brown hair and his eyes would light up with delighted amazement as he saw reflected there the man in long sleeves with folded newspaper, carrying so effortlessly that magnificent chest. God, he was beautiful. God, he was strong. And he would turn with an exaggerated elegance and bow to the beautiful women that went by and turn with his still shining eyes to see if I had seen. A few of the women smiled. But it was sadder than it should have been to see the women he was saluting or that he had intended to charm hurry away with alarm, their eyes looking for a place to flee from a man they must have thought crazy. Even before we reached Inn and Out, I had the feeling that the city, after all, without a knowledge of Blues, might take his exuberance in the wrong spirit and might not be giving him the welcome his sincerity and delight merited. His glances at

39

me asked for approval or comment. I didn't know how to tell him what I had seen.

'And how is Cunaripo?' I asked when we were seated.

'You should be telling me. Is nearly three months I down here. Time,' he said, looking at his watch, a new acquisition. 'Can't find the time to go up since I down here.'

'They should be deep in the football season now,' I said.

'The fellars going to miss you in the middle.'

'They have Porrie,' I said.

'Porrie?' He smiled disdainfully. 'Dribble too much. No speed. Skylark too much. Speed and toughness, that is what you had. When a player see you coming, he know he had to play the ball or clear out the way. Cross Winds going to give us a good tussle this year.'

'We still have Berris and Mervyn. Mosta the other fellars still there.'

'Berris should be playing football down here in the city,' he said. 'I go to the Savannah and watch football there, I see fellars who they call stars playing there. Berris will run rings round them. Berris should be playing real football down here in the big league. But, you know,' he said, almost sadly, 'Berris will never leave Cunaripo. He stays up there. He feel the place so big. And how he will leave? How the world will see him? You lucky, you have education. You travel.' He grinned, 'I watch you, you know. Yes. I watch you.'

We sat in Inn and Out and talked about Berris and the fellars and football and Cunaripo and we drank beers and we talked about the Bazaar. Blues' gestures, his way of speaking, all had the quality of performance with which he had first greeted me. It amused me in the beginning. I took it to be a skill he was displaying, a sort of private demonstration of how accomplished he had become, how at ease he was in the new milieu of the city, and I had waited for him to revert to a more natural tone and manner with me. But, as we went on, it occurred to me that what he was revealing was the new persona which he had settled on for his stay in the city. I accepted his ambition. I accepted that he had a life that had to be acknowledged by me, by the whole world; but I believed that he needed to discard that grotesque performance and seek himself.

'You must come up and see the show,' he said, when we were getting ready to leave. 'Every night we on. Maybe you could even do a story on me. We have people marvelling at the club.' With a smile, he added, 'I doing a new number.'

'Calypso?' I had my own smile.

Just before I left Cunaripo, Phonso had gotten the fellars together and organised a Calypso Tent in the community centre on weekends. 'Make the place bright for Carnival,' Phonso had said, 'Can't leave the place dead so.' That was Phonso: always trying to get something organised, sports, dance, concert, play. He managed to talk a lot of the fellars into singing calypso. A couple Sundays, he took the show to outlying districts. Starved for entertainment, the villagers lapped it up. They treated the fellars royally, like real stars. Blues was one of the hits of the show.

I saw him on the stage of the community centre in Cunaripo one night in the role of calypsonian. He went on stage without a clear tune or thorough lyrics, just a theme, just a chorus: *Chong chiki chong chong*. It was a song about a Chinese man. How Blues did it, I don't know. He kept up with the musicians best way he could, or rather the musicians kept up with him, and he improvised every nonsense that came into his head, coming back to the chorus line: *Chong chiki chong chong kee chong*. He had everybody rolling.

'Not calypso. No,' he said, chuckling, remembering too. 'That is for Cunaripo. No. I breaking iron on my chest.'

I looked at his chest bulging out strong, 'Breaking iron on your chest?'

Seeing me so attentive, he smiled again, 'The Iron Man, that is what they call me.' In his eyes was a mischievous glee, 'Santo, I not suppose to tell anybody, but I will tell you. What they do is heat the iron at a point, break it and rejoin it with solder.' He made a circle with his fingers by way of demonstration. 'When I go on stage and put the iron on my chest and start to strain and put force on it, it is pure acting. A child could break it.' He

41

grinned again. 'The whole thing is one big act.' To him it was a great joke.

'Look,' he said, 'Lemme show you something.'

He took a wallet from his pocket and from it removed a photograph of himself in leopard skin tights, those with the one strap across the shoulder. His face in the picture was contorted and he was sweating and straining to break a bar of iron across his chest.

'That is me, the Iron Man. Heh heh heh! You can't see it in the photo, but, there,' he pointed to a spot. 'You see where the iron is breaking? No, you can't see the difference. Same colour all over.'

For a moment I was astonished that something like this could be happening. I was even more surprised that Blues should reveal this information to me. After all, it was secret. Why did he tell it to me?

Almost immediately, I realised that Blues was giving me another bit of information. It was this: that he had found Port of Spain out. The city was a lie, a sham, a con. It was appearance. It was in no way superior to him.

'You know what they want me to do?' He smiled as a man superior to everybody. He was taking another photograph from his wallet.

'Look at this one. This is Marcia. Dancer. Lovely woman, eh?'

Marcia was a shapely, big-boned creature with her long limbs growing immodestly out of the shiniest and flimsiest costume. She had big, big eyes of the most amazing softness.

'Yours?' I asked, when I could tug my eyes away from her figure.

'No no no!' he cried. But he was smiling with sufficient ambivalence to leave me in doubt. 'No. She is the queen of the band.'

'Which band?'

'That's what I'm telling you about. Paloma night club is bringing out a Carnival band. *The Rise of the Monguls*. They want me to play the king, Attila the Hun.'

42

'The king? You?'

He was smiling. 'All the girls from the club will be there. Dancers, tourists, everybody. Why don't you come and play with us? Everybody does have a real good time. Woman like peas.'

'Play with you? These things cost money,' I said. 'Plenty money. I hope you know what you getting yourself in.'

My voice must have been a little stern. I saw a shadow of hurt cross his sculptured face, and for a moment I could feel him struggling to compose himself.

'What happen, Santo? You think I can't handle myself in this town?' A note of reproach had leaked into his voice. 'Anyhow, you always take me for a joker'.

'Blues ... ' I began.

'Yes?' Now it was he who was stern. 'Yes. You always take me for a joker.'

'Is just ... Is just that with me ... With rent to pay and all my expenses, with my salary, I can't afford to play mas'.'

'I have to play. They depending on me.'

'But, can you afford it, Blues?'

'But that is the whole point, Santo. A man don't play a masquerade he can afford. Anyhow, they depending on me.'

'Let me hear that again.'

We were both smiling now.

'If I could afford a mas', then I don't have to play it. You don't see, Santo. I have to show them.'

'Show who?'

'All those people in the club. They look up to me you know. I can't back out now.'

'You right,' I said, 'you know the situation.' I wasn't smiling now. 'Anyhow, watch yourself. Don't make them stick you with the most expensive costume.'

He patted me on the shoulder. In his eyes was a mischievous twinkle, 'Santo, I know how to live. Don't frighten.'

I wasn't convinced that Blues was in command of the situation. I had known many masquerade players who spent their life in debt. I had a feeling that he would find himself out of his depth in that band; but, I had already misjudged him. To lay too great a caution upon him now was to suggest that he didn't know what he was doing. I felt that I had said enough.

Against my protests that we at least split the bill, he paid it all, and we came out into the sunlight of Frederick Street.

'So where can I find you?' I asked. 'What's your address?' For a moment he hesitated.

'Don't forget to come up to Paloma night club,' he said. 'Any night. Just ask at the door for me. And come alone,' he added. 'It have plenty nice woman up there. Heh heh heh.'

We parted there in front of Inn and Out. As I watched him straighten himself and step off with his contrived gentility, I wished there was some more substantial way in which I could help. I hoped that he would be able to pay the price of the masquerade that he couldn't afford but was convinced that he had to play. I wanted to say something to him, but somehow I didn't feel I had the right. Maybe he really knew how to live.

THE COWARD

With his hair brushed and parted, Blues stood on The Drag with his tie and his neatness and his new platform shoes and watched, transfixed, the cavalcade of black princes crowned with tall hair go by on majestic stilts, their bodies wrapped in banners, the flagpole of their fists punching the skies, their volcanic shouts of 'Power!' thundering across the hillsides. He watched black queens, their heads wreathed in flowers, their rhythmic skirts stretched across undulating hips, dancing through clouds. He saw warriors misted in incense, with breastplates of ebony and berets of Cuban fighters marching through the city with the machine guns of anger and grenades of pride. He watched wave upon wave of black people, so tall, bending their heads down to pass below the electric wires hanging across the streets.

'You know where they going,' an old African man said with a broken smile. He was standing next to Blues and Blues saw the light shining in his eyes. 'Africa. They going to Africa.'

Mr Cabral, a tall fair-skinned mulatto who had a big position at the Royal Bank, where Blues worked as a Security Guard, was also smiling. He was looking at Blues, 'You going with them?' It was the first time he had spoken to Blues.

Blues started to smile, but the drums were beating in his head.

'I have to take up work at three,' he said, looking at his watch.

45

'Want to go to Africa with them?' Cabral said, smiling. Blues smiled too.

'Is Africa they going,' the old man said looking around gleefully.

'You can't go to Africa with them. Those who going aint have no work to do,' Mr Cabral said.

'I just watching,' Blues said.

'Be careful,' Mr Cabral said. 'It might have violence.'

'From just marching.'

'Wherever it have so much people, look out for violence. As a security man, you should know that. You don't see the police vans behind them.'

And indeed, when Blues looked he saw cruising behind them two van loads of policemen. But the drums were beating in his head, and he set off behind them.

Walking with his tall upright self-admiring walk, with his chest stuck out, and keeping on the pavement, Blues followed them down the street, past show windows with mannequins with blonde hair modelling tweed jackets and Parisian blouses. In the mirror of a display window, he caught a glimpse of himself and realised with a shock that suddenly he didn't look so tall, that he wasn't cool at all, that his tie was a rope around his neck and where was the crown of his hair? He followed them past grape and apple vendors and Indian charioteers standing in carts beheading green coconuts, past the forbidding silence of imperial banks and the grey walled fortress of the Police Headquarters, and policemen at attention in front of the parliament building, and with the drums beating still in his head, he flowed with them into Woodford Square where the grass lay down panting in the huge shadow of a samaan tree at the table of whose roots vagrants with serene indifference to the noises around them were preparing a meal seasoned with the salt of their tears. He saw Baptist mothers ringing bells as they spun among bowls of golden marigold and the pillars of lighted candles while the white frocked sisters hummed and swayed in the stormy wind of the descending Spirit.

And then Blues was standing in front of the bandstand among thousands where, surrounded by Nubian standard bearers, holding up flags of black, red and green, black leaders with necklaces of clenched black fists and *dashikis* covered with maps of Africa roared for freedom. He could smell the city burning. He saw Africa blaze beautiful through the gauze of a dream. He heard that he had another name, a real name, that his name was not his name. That he was never a slave. That he was a captive who had struggled in this strange land to give it a soul. You are not a footnote in the whiteman history. He heard that he was maker of a new history.

'You make this land,' the leader said 'Yes, you. You black, knotty head, majestic people. Watch the movements around you. Listen! The music, the language, is all your creation. And look how you live. But if I tell you these things, if I talk, they will lock me up, they will throw me in jail. They will say I am a rabble rouser rousing the people out of their contentment. So I not going to talk.'

'The leader is not going to talk,' another of the leaders shouted.

'Let him talk,' the crowd shouted.

'I know you want me to talk,' said the leader, 'But, I don't want to talk. I want the facts to talk. I want you to see. I want you to touch and to smell.'

'*Power*!' Cried the people. 'Power! Pow-er!'

The leader held up his hands, 'We going to Shanty town to see.'

'We are going to walk with black dignity and black pride and in black peace,' One of the leaders shouted. 'We are not to provoke the police.'

In the glare of the brilliant battering heat Blues followed them down to Shanty Town, to see black emperors stepping out of their palaces of cardboard into the ooze of the suffocating vapours of decay to contest with squalling *corbeaux* and mangy stray dogs the rights to the treasures in the unmined mountains of refuse dumped upon their doorsteps.

'Come and see how they live!' another leader cried.

And still carrying the ferocious stink of Shanty Town on his clothes he marched with them through Woodbrook and

47

Coblentz into the dream of Elleslie Park where under the noiseless sunshine children rode bicycles and flew model aeroplanes in front of residences fenced with wrought iron and doberman dogs. And still in the dream, he walked under the shaded samaan trees to that club where the only black people permitted, they said, was the bartender and a negro doctor knighted by the queen.

'If I talk you will not believe,' said the leader. 'If I talk it will be too much. I have only one sentence to speak. This, Brothers and Sisters is the year nineteen hundred and seventy. This, Brothers and Sisters is an independent country. This my beautiful people is taking place under the regime of a government that you have voted for.'

Blues found himself trembling. He felt his head buzzing. The drums were filling his belly. He looked at his watch. It was nearly three. He had to get to the bank to do his security. He began to look for a place to run. He felt he wasn't safe. He began pushing his way through the crowd. 'Take it easy, Brother,' People were saying, but he was elbowing people out of his way. 'Take it easy.'

I was moving closer to get a better look at the speakers. He saw me. We came face to face.

'Don't tell me you in this thing, Santo,' he said with a grimace of pain.

'I come to see what's happening,' I said, waving my notebook. 'I covering the demonstrations for *The Standard*.'

'And they send you? Anyhow, if you working work. Keep your distance and write your story, but don't get involved. I going. Just write your story and keep out of this. It going to have plenty trouble here.'

'You surprise me,' I said. 'I thought you would be a supporter. People here fighting for their rights, you know. For their dignity.'

'Santo, people will get kill in this thing.'

'This is people fighting for their name, for justice.'

'You could imagine what would happen if I try to look for justice, for dignity. I try to get back my name, and all the labour they owe me. You could imagine what will happen if I try to get my language back? Santo, you and all these people joking. You

48

hear me. You all just talking but you don't understand. I listen to every speech and not one of them understand the price they asking. People will get kill.'

'And you frighten?' I said coldly. 'Frighten to die?'

'Yes, Santo,' he said. 'Yes.' Suddenly his face was very sad. 'But I aint frighten to dead. I frighten I kill somebody. Let it go. Let them go with what they thief. Let them keep it.'

'And we will go to sleep. Leave things just so and go back to sleep?'

I thought he was going to strike me, so fierce were his eyes. Instead he said softly, 'Yes. But I don't know how sound a sleep it will be.'

THE FIRE EATER'S RETURN

In the half light of the night his smile came out like the desperate grimace of a hungry, big-headed grey cat, something between a snarl and a smile, and for a moment I could not tell whether his intention was to entreat or to attack. I shifted my body so as to be sideways to him so I could parry his blow or launch my own counter-offensive if he intended to be hostile. The smile broadened. It was Blues.

Blues no longer exuded his usual air of grandeur. His face had a bleached, grey look, like he wasn't getting enough sleep or proper food to eat. And though he was still neat, with his shirt tucked into his trousers and his sleeves buttoned down at the wrist, his chest had caved in, and the sparkle had gone out of his eyes.

'God, I glad to see you!' he said.

Seeing me looking at him, he reached for the camouflage of a smile; but, I could see behind that smile that Blues had come face to face with a most formidable reality, and his optimism that he would conquer the world of the city with his own cunning and charm and his pretence at gentility had finally run out.

'This is my lady,' he said, indicating the woman at his side. I had been so focused on Blues that I had not made any connection between him and the woman who had followed him as he dodged his way through the traffic to cross the street.

I now looked into a beautiful, ravished face with large, beady eyes of a frightening intensity. Her thin body was folded in a long, African-print dress and her small head was wrapped in a headtie of the same cloth. 'I am Santo,' I said.

She made no attempt to shake my hand, and she mumbled something and moved a little closer to Blues.

'I didn't get your name,' I said.

'Ayesha,' she said, with such surprising hostility that I wondered what wrong I had done her.

I remembered then that I had seen her with Blues at Carnival. It was the Tuesday. The last band had left the Savannah stage where it had gone to be judged for Band of the Year competition. Around the Savannah the disc jockeys were belting out calypsos over their sound systems. Young people were assembling for their last lap, their last dance. Parents were taking children home. On the street were strewn bits of costume, suddenly superfluous for masqueraders. A sword there, a cape of a Ghengis Khan warrior, the headpiece of a Viking, a pair of wings of an angel, a warrior's lance, a devil's tail. Blues had apparently collected from these bits and pieces and made himself a costume and he was rushing with his costume into the band, moving with a frenzied reckless dancing, in one hand a lance, the other hand keeping the Viking's headpiece securely on his head. His angel's wings sticking out from beneath his arms. And he was going, going with a ferocious energy. In the half light of the fading evening, I caught a glimpse of his face from where I was standing. There was no humour on it. It was a tortured mask with his grin. The sole of one shoe had come loose and was flapping and it gave to his otherwise frenzied display a sort of pathetic and awesome sadness. Authentic masqueraders cleared the way for him. In fact, he cleared his own way, and those glimpsing this madness, feeling the brush of his wings and fearing danger from his lance, got out of his way. Behind him, running to keep up with him was this same woman, dressed in the same clothes. I suspect she was trying to restrain him. But he wasn't taking her on. From where I stood I saw Blues plunge himself into the band and plough his way through with his irresistible and absolutely frightening and intimidating frenzy. No one tried to stop him. The whole thing lasted perhaps not a

51

minute and I stood and watched it. I thought of rushing forward and restraining him. I thought Blues had gone mad. If he saw me then, if he saw that I had seen him in this way, the shame would kill him. But it was more than that. In my cowardice I hid from him. I was sure that something violent would take place. Next day I looked at the newspapers to see if they had reported the incident. There was nothing.

Now he was here before me.

'Well, let's go and have a beer,' I said. 'It's years I aint see you.'

'Yes. Let's go and siddown somewhere. Where?' He looked at me for guidance. And in that look, I saw for the first time since knowing Blues a look of defeat, of surprise, of disappointment, of someone let down and ashamed.

We went to an upstairs place right there on Independence Square and he was the first to sit down, dropping into his chair like a weight sinking into a river.

'Sit down,' he said to Ayesha and she drew her chair close to his and sat down.

'How's things?' I asked. It was really a formality.

'Hard,' he said. 'Things hard. Things not good. They say they have a recession, they have to lay off people ...'

'Why you don't get a job for him?' Ayesha said accusingly. 'You's a big editor.'

'Ayesha,' Blues said, lifting his voice tiredly. 'What you going on with that for?'

'But, you want a job,' she said. 'And he is your friend. Your big friend.'

Blues was speaking almost to himself, his voice was so low, 'I was working with Atlas Security. You working in this job. You have to stand up whole day. You can't sit down. You have to be there to watch everybody, to look at everything. And what I there for. I have this gun on my waist. I have this gun and you know it have times when I say to myself, why you don't stick up the cashier. Why you don't rob the bank.'

'And you spending money so free with your big friends. Always so free with money,' Ayesha said, accusingly.

And Blues: 'Is not the money alone. Is everything. Is life. Is how Kelly dead. How in the revolution he go up on the Hills and how they bring him down with his head blown away. Kelly was there in Cunaripo playing good good football. He was nearly as good as Berris, you know. And what he get shoot for? People don't even remember him. Is the love, Santo. Is how people don't care.'

'And all this time you spending money like you have money,' Ayesha said, addressing him. She turned to me, 'You never wonder where he getting money from? You see him spending, carrying girls to the beach, going and sit down in restaurant. You was his friend. You never tell him nothing?'

'So what I protecting with that gun?' I ask. 'So I give them they gun and their uniform otherwise any day I would stick up the bank.'

The waitress came around for our order.

'What you having?' I asked Ayesha.

She looked dumbly at me.

'You not taking a beer?' Blues asked her.

'No. I don't want no beer.'

'What you want?'

'I don't want nothing.'

I looked at Blues.

'Don't worry with her, eh Santo.' And, to Ayesha, 'Ayesha, Santo is my friend, from Cunaripo. Is nearly twenty years I know him. Is a long time. I learn a lot from him.'

'So, you see what he come to,' Ayesha said to me. 'You was his model. You know he take you for his model. He was trying to follow you.'

'I will take a guinness,' Blues said.

'And bring a beer for me. A guinness and a beer,' I said to the waitress.

'Ayesha,' Blues pleaded. He was sort of embarrassed for me, 'Ayesha, is twenty years I know Santo.'

'And you think Santo know you?' She was addressing me now. 'You know Blues? Blues like to be a big man, a big gentleman. Blues like people to like him. He want to be somebody. He spend

53

his money free. He don't complain. Nobody don't ever think about him. Is just his hard luck now. You meet and you drink and you talk. You know anything about Blues? And he live in a dream, he live in a dream. And is not until somebody go mad or kill somebody that you half wake up and see that that is where it was going all the time.'

'Ayesha, I tired tell you. Don't talk that talk.' But Ayesha was on her way to the bathroom.

'I know its rough,' I said.

'They beat me, Santo.' There was a timbre of surprise in his voice. 'I come in town. I come to this city. I was never lazy. I was always doing something.'

I knew Blues was desperate. I had seventy dollars on me. I gave him fifty. He just put it in his pocket without saying anything. I took out my cigarettes and gave him one. I lit it for him.

We were both smoking silently when Ayesha returned.

'Take something,' I begged her.

She took a pull off Blues' cigarette. She still didn't want to have anything to do with me.

'Don't worry with Ayesha, you know,' Blues said. 'She does say anything. She have a hot mouth. Look, I tell her. I say, Girl, if anybody is to blame for anything is me. Is me.' He struck his chest. 'I can't blame anybody else. Is just that, that I thought I did know how to live. You know what I mean, Santo? I don't want no set of things, she neither. We don't want no set of things, eh, Ayesha.'

Ayesha took one of his hands, 'Let's go,' she said. 'We going.' She began to get up.

'I play the arse a lot too, you know,' Blues said, with his first smile for the evening.

'Yes,' I said, with my own smile. I was thinking of his performance, of his affectation. I was thinking of his coming down here in the city, the masquerade, Attila, the women.

'No.' Ayesha screamed. 'No.' She really was intent on opposing me. 'No. You didn't play the arse more than anybody. You was stupid, but you wasn't more stupid than anybody. You

54

wanted to be a gentleman.'

'Yes, I thought it was so easy. The clothes, the walk, I had everything. I thought I was fooling them,' Blues said. 'They was the ones fooling me. I was the fool.'

'People have to find their own truth,' I said. 'Everybody.'

'You shoulda tell him that long ago,' Ayesha said. 'Why you didn't tell him that?'

'People have to live their own life,' I said.

'Why you didn't tell him that this was shit? He was watching you.'

Blues was watching me now.

'I suppose that I was a believer too,' I said.

Nobody said anything.

'Give me an orange juice,' Ayesha said.

Neither Blues nor I said anything lest we rouse Ayesha who sat like a trigger sipping the orange juice.

'About the job,' I said, when we were ready to leave, 'I don't know what they will have. But, come and see me sometime next week. That will give me some time to see if I could see somebody who know somebody who you could talk to for a job. Make sure and come, you know. Ayesha, see that he come.'

'Okay. And thanks,' he said, talking about the money. 'You save my life today.'

But, no. I did not save his life.

Blues did not turn up the next week as I expected him to. I saw him about a month later as I was coming out of the newsroom. He looked a bit better but wasted, hard. He was wearing a long African dress over his trousers. A silver bracelet was on his wrist and his head was bound with a red cloth. He was wearing sandals. Ayesha walked a few paces behind him. He looked very serious, and he was bowing to everyone on the way. 'Peace Brother. Peace and love. Peace sister.'

'I thought you say you would come to see me,' I said.

'The black race is under threat. They are stealing our dreams, our rhythms. Santo,' he said seriously, 'you have to stop sleeping. What you doing with yourself? You have to get out the rat race. People have to care, Santo. People have to care about people.'

'Where you going now? Come, let's take a beer.'

'Sorry. I have to go to the Square. I preach there. I counsel the sufferers.'

'And you, how do you live, man?'

'We take up a collection. A few dollars to buy candles, get something to eat.'

'Okay, then. Next time.'

Then, a few months ago he came into the office of the newsroom of *The Standard*. He was dressed in leopard skin tights, his head was bound with a single golden band across his forehead, a bar of iron on his shoulder. He looked greying, paunchy. Ayesha was with him. She had some handbills. She was in the same costume of the African woman. She was handing out the handbills, things that they had written up and had xeroxed.

THE RETURN OF THE IRON MAN

FIRE EATING, BOTTLE DANCING AND OTHER OCCULT ACTIVITIES

GRAND DEMONSTRATION IN WOODFORD SQUARE

ADMISSION FREE. GIVE WHAT YOU CAN AFFORD

He wanted me to write a story on him. It was a big thing he was planning. All the newspapers will be there, he said. He had spoken to television, the radio stations. The Bomb will be there. He wanted me to do a story on him so that it would appear on the day of the event and he wanted me to send a cameraman to cover it.

'It will be the greatest thing in Port of Spain,' he said.

Ayesha stood silent watching him, watching me.

I took the details of the show and I wrote the story. I had a lot of questions, however.

Twenty years ago Blues came to Port of Spain with an acrobatic troupe from Cunaripo, bottle dancing and eating fire. Today he returns this time to Woodford Square to give the public a treat with his superhuman feats, defying pain and banishing suffering.

I wrote the story and gave it to the editor. He didn't publish it. Another story on him appeared in one of the weekly papers. It made Blues look comical. My story would have given a better perspective on Blues.

That Friday morning he came to the office, he and Ayesha.

'I see the *Evening News* write something. *The Express* had something. But, nothing from *The Standard*.'

'Your friend,' Ayesha said, sardonically.

'I write the story, but they didn't use it.'

'You sending somebody today? Why you don't come and cover it? I see your name on all kindsa articles. If you cover it, people bound to read it.'

'Okay,' I said. 'Okay. Look. Today is parliament. I have to cover the budget debate. That is my assignment. I don't know if I will be able to get away. But, I promise you, I will get a photographer and a reporter to come. It's a promise.'

'Okay,' he said and shook hands. 'I sorry we aint have time for a beer. But, with these things you have to go and see bout everything for yourself.'

'So you stop preaching, or what?'

'Santo, the world today is gimmick. People want something more spectacular than words, something more grand. Faith needs spectacle.' The words had popped out of him spontaneously, even he seemed surprised by them, and impressed.

When he and Ayesha left, the reporters in the newsroom were giggling. 'Santo, you have some real strange friends.'

When I came back from covering parliament that evening, Gordon, the fellow who I had asked to cover the Blues story for me said to me, 'You know I have something to tell you. But what it is slip me.' He was hurrying out of the newsroom. His wife was waiting on him. 'Oh, I know now,' he called out from the doorway. 'You remember that crazy fellar, your friend who was in the newsroom this morning with that thin African woman. Well, he catch himself afire in the square.'

'How you mean catch himself afire?'

'You know these fire eaters does pour some gasolene in their mouth and then light a match and blow out fire. Well it look like this fellar wanted to be so spectacular. Is like he drink a whole pint of gas and when he light it, poof! Was a ball of blazing fire. If you see the great picture Chandler get of it. Want to see it?'

I didn't want to see it.

'That wasn't the fellar you had a story on sometime last week?' the editor asked.

'Yes, I gave it in. But you didn't use it.'

'Well, we running it.'

Next day they had my story in the paper with pictures of Blues with flames pouring out of his mouth and they had a big headline: THE RETURN OF THE FIRE EATER and below that, The Fire Eater Eats His Last.

CALL ME 'MISS ROSS' FOR NOW

Late already for the start of the Village Council meeting, Miss Ross left her friend Fedosia Aguillera dressing for the dance and in the last sunlight of the dying September evening hurried up the street to the Community Centre. Each short padding step of her parrot-toed feet released victorious rhythms from the wondrous springs of a body that at age forty-seven could still make the men at the corner forget how to breathe. When she got there she found the building locked and not a soul present. She felt like just turning around and going back home and dressing up and going to the fete with Fedosia, though she didn't like the idea of two big women alone leaving Cunaripo and going eleven miles to a fete in Arima without even one man between them; but, she turned from that madness, reminding herself that for years she was the first one to arrive at these meetings. This didn't console her. And she turned, as if to demonstrate to herself her indispensability, into the street at the side of the Centre to go and get Fitzroy the caretaker to come and open the building, hoping that at this hour on a Friday evening, with the club hot with gambling, she would find him home, still fresh in her mind the time he left with the key in his pocket and went seventeen miles to Mamoral to gamble and they had to keep the meeting underneath the school house. Mr Rivers had wanted to get rid of him right away, but she and Norma had begged for him. Not even Norma was here now.

knew her name. 'I let him sleep,' said not with apology but with triumph.

Miss Ross felt she should say something. She said, 'I don't see you at the Village Council meetings. The Council is for everybody, you know.'

'He,' she said, pointing in the direction of the sleeping Fitzroy, 'always promising to bring me. I will be glad to come. In Orosco we used to have concerts. I used to sing. You don't know I went up on Scouting for Talent?'

'Then you must come,' Miss Ross said.

Miss Ross was still smiling as she crossed to the Community Centre.

Norma's two teenaged daughters and Elsie's one were returning from the river, laughing, chatting, their wet t-shirts sticking to their bare bodies. No one else was around. She looked at the standpipe nearby. The tap was opened to its fullest. There was no water. She went and screwed the tap shut, then she mounted the steps and unlocked the door of the Community Centre.

Someone had been sweeping the floor and had left the task unfinished and the broom resting on a mound of rubbish in the middle of the hall. Miss Ross took up the broom and started to sweep. As she was sweeping, her mind settled on Fitzroy. She imagined him sleeping, half naked, perspiring, totally at peace, his body thrown across the bed, loosely, secure in the knowledge that his woman wouldn't wake him unless she was sure that the house was burning down. That was his charm, his luck: that trust, belief that he was so beautiful that people would want to protect him.

There was a time, about a year after he had come back from Canada, where he had gone for a year as a farm labourer, when he used to come into the Post Office regularly. He used to gamble a lot in those days. Most times when he lost, he would come next day to the Post Office and talk to her about the piece of land behind the river where he was planting pumpkins and sweet peppers and about the board house he was building, and she would tell him about the Council and

62

the problems of getting the people together. They used to talk a lot, and she would look forward to his coming, and sometimes she'd have a glass of orange juice for him, and sometimes he would bring a pumpkin or some ochroes from his garden. He didn't look settled. One day he'd be talking about wanting to leave the village, about getting a job, of applying to be a bus conductor or a post man; next day he would be saying how sweet it was to be his own boss, planting his vegetables and catching an iguana and making a cook with the fellars and going about gambling.

One day he came into the Post Office, seeking a letter. He had applied to become a security guard at one of the big government secondary schools. She had gone to the cupboard to check for his letter, and had her back turned to him. She heard the silence and thought that he was looking at someone passing in the street and realised, only when she turned round, that it was her he was watching.

'Miss Ross,' he said. 'You really looking good these days, you know. What it is you eating?'

'Thank you,' she said, stiffly, pretending not to notice the section of her body he was admiring. She didn't want to encourage him. He had never stepped out of line with her before. There were men who came in, who looked her over and made what they called rough jokes with her, but these were closer to her age. He wasn't one of them.

'I mean it,' he said. 'You really looking good.'

She tried to make her face serious then; but, instead of feeling outraged, she felt an alarm as if the front of her blouse had got undone and her breasts were showing. For one eternal moment they looked at each other with the fiction of casualness, he, without the language to go further, she, without the power to compose herself, feeling more alarm about what she had revealed about herself than about what he was saying.

'I mean it,' he said.

There was no letter for him, and he went away.

That night she went to sleep and dreamed of flying. She was standing under the moon and a bull, grazing in the savannah,

63

suddenly began to run towards her. She was rooted to the spot, and she took out a letter from the cupboard in the Post Office, and tried to shoo it way. It came hurtling towards her with its head lowered and its horns showing and at the very last minute the letter opened into a parachute and she jumped up and began to fly away.

'What man you trying to get away from?' Fedosia asked her, when she told her the dream.

'Man?' she told Fedosia. 'I too old for that.'

The day after her dream, he returned to the Post Office. She had put on a going-out dress and had combed back her hair, the way she had it sometimes when she went to church. She could see him looking at her, his eyes more watchful, as if he needed to measure and assess what had happened two days earlier. She stood his quiet scrutiny within the fiction of their nonchalance, going to the cupboard to look for his letter which she knew wasn't there, since she had checked for it earlier, returning empty handed, trying to sound casual, consoling, 'Like these people forget you, boy.' But, she could hear that her own voice was different.

'Miss Ross, you know you really looking good,' he said.

'Is that so? Maybe is the dress I have on.'

He had a way of smiling that stretched his mouth and filled his eyes, 'I mean it,' he said. 'Every day you looking more good.'

'Boy, what you doing? You making a move on me? You don't realise I know you since you's a little boy.'

'Little boys does get big, Miss Ross.' And she could feel him watching her with another eye, the male animal eye.

Trying to turn it into a joke, she said, 'Look, I don't know if I able with you, you know.'

That Easter the Village Council organised a Sports meeting and Dance. She went to the Sports dressed in a soft flowered chiffon dress. She felt she was floating. Everybody was looking at her, and Fedosia kept asking her, 'Tell me who he is?' And she kept telling Fedosia, 'Girl, what stupidness you talking?'

She saw him there in an old bus conductor's cap and a jersey with the sleeves cut off. He was running a roulette game under the mango tree at the side of the ground, singing out his pitch with the panache of a born hustler, 'Over here! Over here! Don't be lucky and coward. Bet big to win big! Three to one on horses. Five to one on roses. Eight to one on hearts.' She and Fedosia went over to his game.

'Don't be lucky and coward!' he sang, looking at her, his smile filling his eyes.

Fedosia put down twenty-five cents on roses and Fedosia won. She put another twenty-five cents on roses, but hearts came. Fedosia wanted to keep on betting, but she pulled her away. 'Let's go. Let's go. Don't let him win you back.' And they left, laughing, she and Fedosia. Later, as she and Fedosia were standing looking at the races, he came over and put two cold beers in their hands and went away.

'Miss Ross?' Fedosia said looking at her with astonishment, 'I didn't know you was so brave.'

'I don't know what you talking about.'

That night at the dance in the Community Centre, he came up to where she was sitting with Fedosia and Mr Rivers and some friends Fedosia had invited up from Valencia. Wordlessly, he had stretched out a hand for her to dance and she had taken it. It was a slow number, and he had locked her in an embrace, one arm around her neck, the flat of the other hand resting on the curve of her buttocks, just below her waist, his body pressed scandalously against hers, she on tiptoe, her head barely peeping out above his shoulder. When he let her go, she was gasping for breath and Fedosia was looking at her with something between amusement and satisfaction.

'You see my crosses,' she said to Fedosia, smoothing down the back of her dress. 'The boy have everybody looking at me.'

'Ross, you too damn hypocrite,' Fedosia said. 'You like it.'

'I frighten,' she said. She tried to make it sound like a joke, but she was serious. Afterwards, when he came back to dance, she rested a hand on his shoulder to keep him at a safe distance, and they struggled silently with each other, he trying to get closer, and she resisting silently.

One day after that, he came to the Post Office. He still

65

hadn't received a reply to his application. 'Miss Ross?' he asked. 'What is your name?'

'You don't know my name?'

'Well, everybody call you "Miss Ross". You don't have another name?'

'Fitzroy,' she said. 'If you come for letters, I don't have any for you today.'

'All these years I know you, I never hear anybody call you by your other name. What is it people call you, who don't call you "Miss Ross"?'

'What you want to know that for?' But, she found herself rubbing her perspiring hands against the front of her dress.

'I just want to know. For myself,' he said.

Miss Ross felt herself in need of time. 'Boy,' she said, 'I find you going too far.'

'Really, what name to call you?'

'Fitzroy,' she said, 'Call me "Miss Ross"' But, seeing the disappointment cross his face, she added, 'For now.'

And now, sweeping the floor of the Community Centre Miss Ross was remembering how already as a girl, the villagers had started to call her 'Miss Ross'. 'Miss', not so much the acknowledgement of spinsterhood, as a title of respect conferred on those they wished to set apart from the ordinary, a distinction she had earned from the age of fifteen when she began running single-handedly a private school for pre-school children. And she was beautiful. So, by the time she became post mistress, her distance from the villagers had already been established, and even the most audacious and handsome of their young men trembled to talk to her, realising, as she did, that she was too precious to end up becoming the wife of an estate labourer or a wood worker; and she was left with the sense of being a fairy tale princess whose suitors would come from foreign parts, past the marshes of ignorance and the ogres of the unbelievable boredom to rescue her from the lazy evenings of the forgotten village on the outskirts of Cunaripo.

And they came, a procession of them, teachers and forest rangers and agricultural assistants and ward officers, young men posted to the district on government business, on the steed of motorcycles to make their business the pretty post mistress who was also secretary of the Village Council, on the church committee, in the Credit Union, the Women's group, the handicraft society. They whispered their coarse jokes and the urgent priority of their desires while her mother, who was going blind, smiled politely out of cloudy eyes, happy to see such interest expressed from such official quarters in her daughter; while the villagers looked on from the distance of their closeness, their mouths stuffed with gossip every time she took a taxi, the ubiquity of their eyes reminding her that she, unlike their adolescent sisters entering confidently from pregnancy into womanhood, had a reputation to guard.

Always the men she fell for were the most forceful, if not the most handsome, those who managed to maintain a sense of performance, a sense of play, while they snuggled closer to her, they both conniving in the pretence that nothing remarkable was happening, in this way neither of them having to claim responsibility, she, allowing herself to be overpowered just to the degree that she thought it convenient to allow herself and to bring the relationship to a halt when she was tired of the role of feminine helplessness which was essential for its survival. But, there were the quiet ones, sly, her mother called them, who came snaking into her heart, demanding her complete attention while themselves keeping the male vault of their person locked away even to themselves, making her in the beginning feel alive and wanted, but this one would forget to tell her that he was married, or, that one, that he was engaged or being transferred to another part of the island. And there was Gordon who remained forever a stranger, polite, thoughtful, studied, as if it would kill him to give himself on his own, to commit himself for himself, always on guard, always parrying, dishing out his tenderness in doses that were never enough to commit him. They quarrelled, they fell out, they made up, and when she realised that that commitment would only occur if it was forced upon him, if he had no alternative, she had already shown too much of herself,

67

been too open with him to now turn around and play tricks. She couldn't go on like that. She had surrendered. And she was suddenly so tired, all she wanted was for somebody to hug her, that was all. But suddenly the officers coming to the district were getting younger, though that was a delight, not a bother to Fedosia who had come back from Tunupuna to live in the big house that her brother had recently renovated, whose advice to her was, 'You have a chance to train them young.' But she had something to uphold. And, tired of fending off the advances of elderly County Councillors and politicians at those meetings at which she represented the village of Cunaripo, and embarrassed at going out with Fedosia and one of her young fellars, she looked again at the village. The only man there with substance enough to interest her was Vincente Aguillera, Fedosia's elder brother. Vincente, with his broad, flat face and his small hawk's nose and his eyes filled with unease, as if he was engaged in calculating the price he would be called upon to pay for anything more than a casual friendship. He had risen from owning a bull in the old days to having a tractor with which to pull logs from the forest. With wood scarce, he had begun to concentrate on establishing a poultry farm. He was a heavy, silent man, strong, muscular still from his days of working the bull, who had had an eye on her from their younger days, but who had kept a respectful distance, not wanting to contend with the forest rangers and the ward officers and the government men who flocked around her.

Fedosia told her one day, 'He always talking about you. You so polite and intelligent and nice. Not like me.'

'He tell you this to tell me?' she asked Fedosia.

'No. He could talk for himself. But the way he talk, you is the exact woman for him. And, I agree. Give him a chance. Marry him.'

Once she invited him to a dance in the Community Centre. It wasn't really a personal invitation. She was secretary of the Village Council then, and was inviting everybody. He was cautious, shy. He said he didn't know if he could still dance;

68

but, yes, he would come, if she promised to dance with him. Of course she would dance with him, she said.

He came to the dance with his cream flannel pants and his flowered shirt and his powerful chest and his shiny brown shoes and his brown felt hat and he brought a bottle of whiskey for the table at which she was sitting with Mr Grannum and Fedosia and a young police corporal who had come with Fedosia. Everybody was having a good time and Mr Grannum was in form, joking with Fedosia about how the young police corporal who was dancing close close with her had her under arrest. Everything was fine, until she started to dance with other men who were not at their table. Right away Vincente started to set up his face and to drink heavier and he nearly got into a row with Mr Grannum for refusing a drink to a friend Mr Grannum had invited to their table. After that he didn't dance again for the night, just sat and drank. When it was time to leave, she and Fedosia had to wake him up.

Afterwards, he came to the Post Office and told her, 'How you could invite me to a dance and you hardly dance with me?'

'But I am in the Village Council, and if people ask me to dance, I have to dance. Is our fete. I wanted everybody to enjoy theyself. Don't tell me you jealous, Vincente.'

He had smiled his hurt smile, as if to say it was okay, but it wasn't okay. She was kinda sorry that he had misunderstood her invitation. She liked Vincente, the softness in him, the part that hurt; but she didn't know if she would want a man who could get so peevish so easily.

'Look, next time, you invite me out. But, not in the village. Let's go somewhere else. Then you'd have me all to yourself.'

'You mean it?'

She meant it.

He invited her to a dance in Arima. He hired a motor car and they went. It was one of those friendly society dances, with men in jackets and ties and women in long dresses. She didn't know anybody at the fete. Vincente felt compelled to buy a bottle of whiskey for their table; and they sat, the two of them, very stiff and proper, the whiskey like a mountain before

69

them. They didn't dance much. Vincente talked about his poultry business, about his eggs and his feeds and his workers and his layers, and all the time she was wondering how was the two of them alone going to finish a whole bottle of whiskey. She tried to have a conversation with Vincente but she felt all the time the need to assure him that her disagreements did not mean disrespect or antagonism. She began to feel stale. She thought drinking more whiskey would make her lively. It got her tipsy. Later, after the dance, they sat on a bench at the bus station, waiting for a taxi, Vincente's arm was around her shoulders. Suddenly she began to cry. She didn't know why she was crying. The tears just poured and poured. In the midst of her distress, Vincente wanted to be assured that it wasn't because of something he had done. She bawled. It didn't work out, things between her and Vincente. They remained friends, that was all. About a year later, he brought a half Indian girl to live with him.

Miss Ross was still sweeping when Mr Rivers came in.

'Miss Ross, where is everybody?'

'Like they late,' she said.

'You see this thing. I don't like it. Is three times already we postpone this meeting in order to get a quorum, and instead of more people coming, the numbers getting less. These people should be here. Myrtle and Benjamin know that today is the meeting. What happen to them? And what you doing sweeping? What we paying a caretaker for?'

'The broom was there, so I just take it up and start to sweep.'

'Who opened the Centre? Fitzroy?' He was looking for something to get vexed about.

'I went for the key,' she said meekly. It vexed her, this meekness, this defensiveness.

'Miss Ross, all you spoiling that boy. All you spoiling Fitzroy. He have his work to do, let him do it.'

She didn't say anything. Her defensiveness had come later, forced upon her because she cared and needed to smooth things over. Others could get vexed. Others could walk out;

but, not she. She had stuck with the Village Council in the hope that she would be able to help people to come together as people, so that they could together decide for their community how to protect and treasure the best in themselves. At her time of life now, she had begun to see life in things, to treasure life, adventure, the boldness. But, she herself wasn't bold.

One Friday Fitzroy had come into the Post Office. He came with a guinness stout wrapped up in a paper. This is for you. She didn't know what to say. He had won at gambling the night before. He was taking a break for he knew the fellars were thirsty to win back. He took out his wallet to show her the neatly stacked bills.

'Miss Ross, you don't like wrestling?'

'I see it on television. It okay. Why?'

'People say is fake, but the licks I see those wrestlers sharing look real enough to me. When Apollon butt a man it look like a real butt to me. I wouldn't like him to rest his head on me.'

Miss Ross was knitting a table mat, something she sometimes did while waiting for people to come into the Post Office. She looked up from her knitting, 'So, what happen? You going in for wrestling now?'

'It have endless excitement,' he said. 'Lots of people go to see it down at the Sports Complex, women, everybody. It real nice. Some of us going tomorrow. You don't want to come?'

Just then the mail van came to deliver letters and to collect the Post Office's mail. She was glad for its coming. It gave her some time to breathe. She gave over her letters, signed the slip to receive those they had brought, and they were gone. She placed the mail bag on the table for sorting, cut the string that tied the mouth of the bag and emptied the contents on the table.

He spoke again, 'We hiring a car. Sylvestre will be driving. He's a safe driver, not like Ruthven. You ever drive with Ruthven?'

'A couple of times, and I reach safe,' she said, her head bent over the table with mail.

'Well, if you have any use for your life, don't go far with Ruthven. That man does get crazy as soon as he get behind a

71

steering wheel. When I in his motor car, I don't blink. When we go to town, we park near the Sports Complex where they have the wrestling, and we go to a little place and sit down and have a beer. It have music there, and sometimes people dancing, but we just go for the beer, and then we go to the wrestling. We stay until the whole programme finish, because we have Sylvestre there with the car to bring us back and we don't have to go and hustle for transportation.'

'Fitzroy,' Miss Ross cut in, 'your letter come.'

'And you don't have to pay,' Fitzroy said. 'It not going to cost you nothing. Let me tell you who going: Moxy and Merle and Julius and me. You will make five. A full load. Two in the front and three in the back, so you wouldn't be getting squeezed. That is another thing with Ruthven. When you see they going to wrestling, seven and eight of them pack up in his little car. And Sylvestre don't speed and he don't drink since he take up with that Adventist girl, so, you safe.

Miss Ross had his letter in her hand and she walked to the counter with it, 'Your letter come,' she said. 'So long you waiting for it, at last it come.'

'And as to eating. We can get roti or accra and float in St James. You don't have to study nothing.'

She had stood there before him, still holding his letter, wanting to tell him how lovely it was for him to invite her and how she wouldn't really mind a little squeeze, how it would be nice to sit in the back seat pressed against him, his arms around her, and later to drink a beer and eat a float and accra. But she was afraid of the adventure. It was the risk, she would see later, of accepting her distinct and individual liberty. That is what it was. She was afraid to be alone, individual, different, set apart and talked about. She knew that people would talk.

'...And it would be Saturday night,' he was saying. 'So you could stay out late. You don't have to work Sunday.'

She wanted to say something, to tell about all the confusing fears inside her and of the joy. Instead she held up the letter before him, and shook her head, putting what she

72

hoped was a smile on her face, 'Here. Here is your letter,' not daring to say anything more for the tears gathering inside her.

'Why?' he asked.

But she turned back to the sorting of the letters and kept her face averted.

'It woulda be a real nice time,' he said.

She didn't answer.

Towards the end of the following week, he returned to the Post Office. He looked tired. No, he looked uneasy. He was speaking too quickly.

'I not bothering with that job, you know. They want me to go for an interview in Port of Spain; but, I change my mind. I don't really want to be standing up in front a school gate every day policing children.'

She felt that she could speak then, 'I don't think that kinda job suit you either.'

'I will stick with the gardening, and if I could get something around here to do, I will take it. The gardening alone can't pay.'

'How was the wrestling?'

'You know, we didn't go again. That same night Sylvestre car decide to give trouble. I dress and waiting. Fellars was in the club gambling; but, I didn't want to gamble. Ruthven was carrying some people to a fete in Orosco, so, I went with them. I really didn't want to gamble.'

'I sorry you miss your wrestling,' she said. 'Anyway, you'll see it on TV. Though, I suppose is not the same thing.'

'No. Is not the same.' He leaned on the counter, 'I have something to tell you. Maybe you know it already. But, I want to tell you anyway.'

'What is this thing you have to tell me?'

'I have a girl,' he said.

Miss Ross put her hands on the counter for support and her head came up slowly and she looked into his eyes.

'I just wanted to tell you,' he said.

'What you want to tell me your business for? I don't own you.'

73

'I wasn't thinking about nothing. I just went in the fete and she was there and we start to dance.'

'So you just went, just so, and get a girl? You see how you lucky.'

His countenance brightened then, 'I just see her there. And you know how these Orosco fellars don't like strangers to meddle with their women. I just see her there and I decide to take a chance. You know, she didn't have nobody either. I was real lucky.'

'I sure she pretty.'

'Yes.'

'And young.'

'I thought she was from Orosco, but she really from Turure.'

'Just so you go and get a young, pretty girl. You see, is a good thing you didn't go to wrestling.'

'She aint have no family, so, I tell her, "Come home with me", and she say, "Okay".'

For the first Miss Ross had felt real alarm, 'So she with you now? At your place?' She tried to keep her voice calm.

'Yes.'

'Just so, you just meet this girl and you invite her to come with you at your place, to stay. Because she say she aint have no family?'

'Not for that alone. I like her too. I wouldn't bring her home, if I didn't like her.'

'Yes. Is true,' Miss Ross said, nodding slowly. 'Yes.'

'She name Eileen. You will see her around.' He pressed his finger tips on the counter, 'You know,' he said, with a kind of sadness, 'You never tell me your name.'

'My name?' she asked, in a dream. 'My name? I thought I tell you "Miss Ross" is my name.'

Miss Ross was finished sweeping when Mr Grannum came in. He was a well-built, almost bald man, with a superior, even mocking air, who seemed to feel that the village was doomed unless he intervened and set things right. He took one look at the empty hall and said, 'Same thing I say. People not interested. We have to get the youths involved.'

'The youths?' Mr Rivers said. 'I just pass the youths playing football in the Savannah.'

Busy, busy, Miss Myrtle, the secretary, came sweeping through the hall, talking all the time, 'All you aint start yet? I have to run. I have a setta work to do home. My daughter just have the baby and everything falling on me.'

'How the baby?' Miss Ross asked.

'Peeing and bawling. The mother have her hands full. Look, Miss Ross, I leaving the book with you. You will have to read the minutes for me. Theophilus aint get his food yet. You know that man when he don't get his food. I leave the pot on the fire. I will come back after I give Theophilus his food.' And with that, she put the secretary's book into Miss Ross' hands and sailed out, swishing her behind with an exaggerated flourish as if it were the twin blades of the motor with which she propelled herself.

As Miss Myrtle was leaving, Fedosia Aguillera strolled in, with her stately sensuous walk, her body held straight, at each step stretching out her leg to its fullest, toes pointed, like a dancer seeking a firm footing on the perilous surface on which she was to perform. Behind her came Mr Grannum's staunch ally, Mr Norman, a thin white-haired man with a mystic and apologetic air about him, 'Sorry to be late,' he said.

Mr Rivers was standing at the doorway looking anxiously at the street. Outside the youths trooped past the Community Centre after their football game, on the way to the river to bathe. Mr Rivers said, 'The youths? The youths. Look at the youths. I wonder what time convenient for them to come to a meeting?'

'In my terms as president, we had all the youths,' Mr Grannum said, proudly, 'Ask Miss Ross. We had a Youth Group. We had a Ladies Group. Ask her.'

Miss Ross really wanted to say nothing but, she felt an obligation to witness to the truth. 'Yes,' she said. 'The Youths used to be here.'

'Excursions, sports meetings. We had a bicycle race from here to Orosco and back. We had a greasy pole competition that brought fellars from as far off as Toco. Look her there, ask her.'

'How we will have a proper sports meeting when we can't even get people to come to an ordinary general meeting?' Mr Rivers said.

'In my term as president we had that problem too, but I solve it. It had a time when a blight hit this Council, when everything we do, nothing coming out right. We try "Each one bring one". We put up posters begging people to come out. We put up a banner across the street. We ask the Catholic priest to preach it in his sermon. Mr Norman had a bicycle and he ride it up and down the village, ringing his bell half an hour before the start of the meeting. Nothing could bring them out. You know what I do? I send out a rumour that I thief money from the Council. I get Norman himself to do it. That get them. They plan a meeting where they was going to try me. When I arrive, the whole Centre full full with people. It had people standing up. They all come out to hear how Grannum thief the Village Council money.'

'You think I should send out a rumour that I thief money?' Mr Rivers asked. He had heard Grannum tell the story before.

'You see how this man ignorant,' Mr Grannum said, glad for an occasion to have a disagreement with Mr Rivers. 'Man, I just telling you about a strategy.'

'I know what,' Mr Norman said. 'Send out a rumour that you closing down the Council.'

'You feel this is a joke, eh, Norman,' Mr Rivers said. And then he added, 'We best had start this meeting. How much people we have here? One … two … three … .'

Five other people had come in.

'We have nine people,' Miss Ross said.

'And what time is it? Twenty to? Well, we will start at seven,' Mr Rivers said.

At twenty past seven, Mr Rivers sat down at the table. To those who were standing around, he said, 'Everybody better come and sit down before more people start to go.'

'Do we have a quorum?' Mr Grannum asked. 'And a returning officer?'

'Sit down everybody, please. Mr Wilkins, you are the treasurer. Sit down here. And you, Miss Ross. You will have to read the minutes. Come here by the table. This is the third time now we waiting on a quorum. We can't keep waiting and waiting. Man wasn't made for the Sabbath.'

'And the returning officer?' Mr Grannum asked.

'How much is a quorum?' asked Mr Norman.

'Mr Grannum, sit down. Everybody, sit down,' Mr Rivers said. In a new tone, one of officialdom, he went on, 'Ladies and gentlemen, I declare this meeting open. The secretary is not here, so I will call upon Miss Ross to read the minutes of our last meeting. Miss Ross.'

When Miss Ross was finished reading the minutes, Mr Wilkins, rose and said, 'I move that the minutes confirm.'

'A seconder,' Mr Rivers cried. 'Who is seconding the minutes. Like nobody else was present at that meeting. What about you, Miss Ross?'

Miss Ross heard herself saying, 'I beg to second the confirmation of the minutes,' and she heard Mr Grannum chuckling. Then she read the one letter, six weeks old, that constituted the correspondence.

Mr Wilkins read the treasurer's report which showed that the Council had a balance of fourteen dollars and eighty cents. This was confirmed and seconded, and then it was time for the election of officers for the new term of the Council. Mr Rivers said that he would act as returning officer.

'All this ceremony.' Mr Rivers said, 'All this semi-demi is all right when you have people functioning, but, if you want to move forward, we have to move.'

Mr Grannum chuckled. 'Ballot paper. We will have to use ballot paper,' he said. 'Miss Ross, give me two pages from your note book.'

'How much people we have here?' Mr Rivers asked. 'Ten people. And we using ballot paper? You can't count? We will do it by a show of hands. What happen, Grannum, you can't count? Nominations open for president.'

'Is not the mathematics, Mr President, it is the secrecy,' Mr Norman said. 'Secret ballot is part of democracy.'

'Nominations open for president,' Mr Rivers said. 'Like all you want to stay here whole night. If you don't want me, just raise your hands and throw me out. You don't have to hide. Everybody here is big people. Nominations open for president.'

Mr Slinger who sometimes did odd jobs for Mr Rivers in his little parlour, and who since he came in had sat down and gone to sleep, roused himself, 'I nominate Mr Rivers,' he said.

Mr Rivers looked at Miss Ross in the silence that followed. He said, 'Like all you really want to stay here whole night.'

'I second Mr Rivers,' Miss Ross said.

'I nominate Mr Norman,' Mr Grannum said.

'Who seconding that? Who seconding Mr Norman?' Mr Rivers asked, and in the same breath, 'Is better somebody move that nominations cease.' He looked at Miss Ross.

Miss Ross got to her feet, 'I move that nominations cease.'

Mr Grannum chuckled loudly. Mr Rivers said, 'Nominations cease.'

Still chuckling, Mr Grannum said, 'Who second that? The procedure is that every motion must have a mover and a seconder.'

'The jurist,' Mr Rivers said. 'The big lawyer. Mr Grannum, I say that nominations cease. I second it. Mr Grannum, please take you seat. You see, this is the kind of confusion that have the Council running backwards.

Mr Grannum said, 'I am standing on a point of order.'

'Let me hear your point of order, counsel,' Mr Rivers said.

'I want to know how Miss Ross could nominate somebody and then move that nominations cease.'

Mr Rivers said, 'You finish your point of order? You finish your advocacy? Well, sit down. I don't want to accuse you of making confusion but, what to call this? A person can move and second any motion. That is what Miss Ross do. She move one motion and she second another motion. Nominations cease,' he said sternly. 'And why is you alone complaining? All in favour of myself as president, show by the raising of hands. Those who too tired to raise their hands, don't raise them. It is just a formality anyway. Good. Unanimous. Now, vice-president.

Mr Slinger nominated Mr Wilkins and Mr Rivers seconded it.

Mr Grannum got up and said, 'I nominate Mr Norman.'

'Who seconding that?' Mr Rivers asked.

As the meeting went on, Miss Ross found herself growing further away from the proceedings. She was thinking of Eileen in Fitzroy's little board house, with her man inside sleeping. She was thinking of her own name, her other name, not 'Miss Ross', the name not spoken for years. She was thinking that she had tried. It was good that she had tried. But she felt that she had held on too long to things that had no use in this time. She wished that she had been more herself, more individual and separate.

In the distance, she heard somebody calling her name. They were nominating her for a position on the executive. Out of the corners of her eyes, she saw Fedosia rise and with her purposeful, slinky, stretching walk, begin to leave. Wait! She realised now. Fedosia was going to the fete in Arima. They were still calling her name. Somebody was seconding the motion to elect her. Fedosia had turned her back and was walking. Miss Ross stood up.

Mr Slinger was saying, 'I beg that nomination cease.'

'I beg to decline,' Miss Ross said.

There was an explosion of silence broken after an eternity by Mr Rivers, 'Miss Ross, what it is you saying? You decline? How you could decline? What will happen if everybody say "I decline"? What will happen if I decline? You want to mash up the Council or what?'

'You, Miss Ross?' Mr Grannum said. 'You? You can't do us that.'

The others were struck speechless, and she saw in Mr

Norman's eyes a look of terror as if he had seen a vision of his own death. And Fedosia was walking away.

'Just a minute,' Miss Ross said, and began to move towards the door and the disappearing Fedosia, feeling with each step a fear circling the pit of her stomach and spreading all over her insides, feeling as if she was stepping into an unknown wilderness, utterly alone. Out the door, she didn't have any voice even to call Fedosia. She began to run. Fedosia heard her and turned. And she ran and she ran with the fear in her that was nothing, she felt, to the terror from which she hoped she had escaped.

THOSE HEAVY CAKES

They used to live in Old Road in Cunaripo; and for him
Christmas was the best time. Best of all was jumping up from
sleep in the last darkness of Christmas morning, with the cocks
crowing, and going into the kitchen where the kerosene lamp was
lit and his mother was up and stirring, and, still in a drowsiness,
hear up the street the far away sounds of the *parang* band – not the
band really, but the thump thump thump of the box bass, the
rhythm bouncing, the thumping getting louder – as it came down
the street and he could hear everything better, the guitar and the
cuatros and the voices singing. Until at last they would be in front
his house, with a quiet fussing, talking soft, soft, as if what they
were doing was a secret and they wanted to surprise his family;
and his family too, with only the one lamp lit in the kitchen,
remaining quiet, not talking, waiting to be surprised; and then
out of the quietness, like magic, the singing would burst out and
day would be breaking and all around cocks would be crowing
and his father would light the other lamp and open the door and
they would come in.

It used to be like it was the whole village that came in, their
house was so small. The only place they had to admit people was
the front room with the floor polished and the centre table
varnished and the balloons hanging low from the low ceiling,
bouncing against the heads that came in. Everybody used to be
in that room for Christmas. And every Christmas his father used
to wait until the people came in to rearrange the furniture to get
more space. Every Christmas was the same thing. It was so

81

packed nobody could move; for somebody to pass in, a whole line of people had to back out, and the only man sitting was the man playing the violin; and brown was the colour: the reddish brown of the mahogany stain of the floor and table, and the lighter brown of the rum and the nearly black brown of the cake and the lustrous polished brown of the skin in which the ham was boiled, with sticks of clove in it; and the smell was varnish and paint and new linoleum from the kitchen; and the sounds was 'Merry Christmas' and laughing and glasses clinking. And afterwards, after the band left, leaving the empty glasses and the rum way down the bottle and the ham deeply wounded and their footprints on the floor, it was like only then, they, his family, could begin to spend Christmas. It was like the music and the singing was the prayer which only after it was finished their meal could begin.

'We have to get a new place,' his father said. 'People can't hold in here.'

'Yes,' his mother said, agreeing. 'We have to get a new place,' busying herself with the cleaning up, 'A bigger place.'

Albert Road was the bigger place. One Christmas after the *parang* band left, his father said, 'This is damn stupidness. This is stupidness. You can't waste money so. You can't waste money buying all these things for people to come in and eat and drink. And when Christmas done, what happen? What? What all this for?' Nobody said anything, not he nor his brother nor his mother.

Next Christmas the band came as usual, with their *shac shacs* shaking and long scraping wail of the violin, came with their hush-hush fussy beginning and his father turned on the light and went to the door and said, 'Come in,' and he moved the centre table to the side and arranged the chairs along the walls, not because the room was so small now, but out of a habit, like if he didn't move the centre table it wasn't Christmas. And the boy looked at him go to the cupboard and bring out two bottles of rum and put them on the table, and after the band played maybe three tunes, his father said to his mother, 'Put something more on the table.' And she brought out bread and sweetbread and cake and two apples and some grapes. And after they had played two more tunes, he said to her, 'Eileen, cut the ham ... cut the ham,' he said, nodding his head, for his mother was a little slow, maybe remembering what he had said about Christmas and wasting.

After the band left, the family was silent. His father picked up an empty rum bottle and said, 'Somebody have to keep it up. You have to give something. You can't let them come in and play and sing and not put out what you have ... anyhow,' he said, 'anyhow, next Christmas. Next Christmas I not buying no ham for them. I going to buy a bottle of rum and put it on the table and when they drink that out, well, that's that. Because you waste all this money, and Christmas is one day, and we have the house to build, and when Christmas done, what happen? What happen? The world go on as usual. 'What we making this great big fuss for?' he said, holding up the knife now to cut the last bit of lean off the hambone. 'Your mother so generous, she give them all the ham. All we people know is fete. That is why we don't have nothing. We fete and fete and when fete done, what? What happen? What is the position?'

Nobody answered him. The boy wanted to say something, to answer something, but he didn't know what. Long afterwards he thought of it. And looking at the people sometimes the thought came to him, they don't have nothing. But somehow this didn't seem true; something was missing.

They had moved to the new house now, in Chaconia Terrace, and for once he had slept late on Christmas morning. He got up with a start, with a sense of hurry and excitement and jumped out of bed, then he remembered that they were not on Albert Road. The living room when he went in was hung with balloons and he could see his face in the floor that he and Marvin had polished and there were the two pictures, sceneries, his father called them, hanging on the walls and whiskey was in the cabinet. He went with Marvin and they opened up their gift, and he got the bicycle at last and Marvin got a flute and skates and a model plane. He took up his bicycle and went into the street. At first he just pushed it. It was funny. He thought he would have been hungry to ride it, but as soon as he got upon it, it was like he had had it all the time. One or two children were riding bicycles and a few were skating and one boy had a kite that wouldn't rise. He rode up the street and he rode back down and he let go one hand. He wanted to let go two hands but he didn't want to appear to be showing off in front of these children.

He parked his bicycle at the side of the house and went in through the front door, pushing aside the curtains gently. His father was in the living room moving around, fixing things, not really fixing them because they were fixed already, but touching them, touching the stereo and straightening the pictures, the sceneries, and touching the vases with the Christmas fern and anthuriums, touching the postcards that hung on a string along one wall, pausing before each object, kinda like he wanted to make sure it looked good, but still wondering if it looked good.

His mother watched him. Her face looked a little strained. She sat by the table where the cake was.

'Who want a piece of cake?' she asked.

Marvin, his brother, didn't want any, but he took a piece. His father also took a piece. After his father tasted it, he screwed up his face. He said, 'This cake light-light. You see those heavy cakes you used to make, heavy, without all this – this fancy recipe you using now, that you used to make without no cook book, without no measuring just the feel from your hands, just with your feelings: those cakes, I coulda eat those cakes.'

She said nothing, and fearing that he had wounded her, he said, 'This not bad, you know ... it not bad, eh?' watching the boy, 'Is just that I ... I coulda eat those heavy cakes.'

He had wandered to the front door and he looked outside, 'Round here quiet, eh,' he said after a while. Then he said, 'Marvin, put on some music.'

'What you want to hear?' Marvin asked him. 'We have some new calypsos that aint sing in the calypso tent yet.'

'What about the *parang* record?'

'That is from since last year,' Marvin said.

'Play it. Play the *parang*,' and spying some cake crumbs on the polished floor, he knelt and took them up with his fingers. He went again to the door and looked outside, 'Listen to this whole street,' he said, 'Listen to it.' He turned away from the door, 'These people aint making not a sound.'

He saw the boy looking at him. He said, 'You get the bike, eh,' trying to sound cheerful, 'I tell you you woulda get it.'

The boy didn't know what to say. His mother was still at the table. Slowly she rose and unfolded a tablecloth and began to cover the cake, 'You coulda eat those heavy cakes?' she asked, her voice cracking under the weight of tears, regretful that after all these years it was something she was hearing for the first time, and with a sadness as if she would never understand the ways of men, of people.

His father stood listening as if she was still speaking, though those were her only words. And as the *parang* music began on stereo the boy could see Christmas morning rise out of the last darkness, with the cocks crowing and the people coming into the lamplight of the little room at Old Road with its smell of new linoleum and varnish; and he thought how this room now would hold so many people.

'Leo, you want a slice of ham?' his mother asked; as if she was waking up, brightly.

He shook his head. Just for something to do, he took up his brother's flute and was going to blow it, but, hearing the other tune begin on the stereo, and feeling like he was going to cry, he put it down and went outside, this time passing through the kitchen and took his bicycle from the side of the house where he had parked it and headed for the street.

GEORGE AND THE
BICYCLE PUMP

When he left work, George walked across the road from the printery, paid for an *Evening News* with a dollar bill, and with just a glance at its headlines, folded the paper and put it in his pocket, while Mary, the vendor, whom he had awakened from a snatched moment of slumber, fumbled almost distractedly among the tins and bottles on her tray for the eighty cents change to give him. He watched her gather with merciless patience, one by one, a set of coins from a small biscuit tin next to her stock of cigarettes, then unearth a twenty-five cents piece from below a jar with dinner mints. She was just reaching into her bosom to continue her search when in a fit of mercy George said 'Give me dinner mints for the balance of the change.'

'You want dinner mints for the change?' she asked, her voice fumbly, appealing, tired, as if the thought, each thought, was a weight to be contemplated before it was lifted; so that George, feeling his own shoulders sag under the burden of her effort, pointed to a bowl of Tobago plums in front of her, 'Look,' he said. 'Give me some of those plums instead.' But, his earlier request had penetrated. With one hand poised suddenly above the jar with the dinner mints, she lifted to him a face with a plea for mercy and a promise of tears. 'All right,' he said, quickly, as if wanting to pull back his last request.

'Give me the dinner mints.' And he watched her count again with tireless exactitude the ten cents and twenty-five cents and five cents pieces, while his hand remained stretched out to receive them; and, she didn't look up until she had extracted, from the store of her inexhaustible patience, the number of dinner mints that equalled the value of the money he was owed; and now, she would count them out again, the coins first, then the sweets, as she pressed them one by one into his open palm, so that he found himself wondering if he would ever get away to get to the Savannah to see his team play their football game.

At last it was over. George dropped the dinner mints and change into the same pocket, crossed the street and, hurrying now, went into the lot at the side of the printery, where he had his bicycle parked. As soon as his eyes fell on the bicycle, he saw that, yes, the pump was missing; and it came to him now, with the calm sadness as at a death that, yes, its absence now was to be explained only by theft. 'They thief my bicycle pump,' he whispered.

Seven weeks ago, when the first pump disappeared from his bicycle, George was certain that one of the fellars from the printery had borrowed it and forgotten to put it back. He was furious. Suppose he had a flat?

'Suppose I had a flat?' he asked at the printery next morning. 'You borrow a pump; you mean is such a hard thing to put it back?' And for most of the day he went about the printery with an air of righteousness and injury, lecturing everybody on responsibility and consideration, and it never occurred to him that the disappearance of his bicycle pump might be explained in any way other, other than the one he had theorised, until Marcos, the supervisor and a friend for the fifteen years he was at the printery, and for the two years before when, as young fellars, they both started out at *The Chronicle*, pulled him aside and said to him, 'George, nobody here aint borrow your bicycle pump.'

'Somebody had to borrow it,' he said to Beulah when he got home that evening. 'The pump just can't walk away.'

'They thief your bicycle pump, George,' Beulah looked up from her sewing, her eyes gleaming with the personal triumph she exuded whenever she suspected that he was in the wrong. 'They thief it!' with a sense of victory, as if it was something she had predicted.

'Thief? Thief my pump? You see you. *Your* mind. Thief is the first thing that come to *your* mind.'

Beulah was sewing a dress for her niece who was getting married in Mamoral in two weeks. She held up the garment and bit off a loose end of thread. 'Where you had it?' she asked, the thread still gripped between her teeth. 'Where you had the pump, George?' She had a talent for making his simplest action appear to be the most criminal stupidity.

'I had it ... ,' George felt like a child. He didn't even want to answer her, 'I had it on the bicycle.'

'You leave your bicycle pump on your bicycle?' She had put down the dress and was looking at him. 'I don't believe you, George.' And with a sigh, she bent her head to her sewing, pressed a foot to the pedal of her foot machine, sending the noise whirring throughout the house. Not another word. She had ended the communication.

But that was Beulah. To her the world outside of Mamoral, where she was born, was a jungle from which her only refuge was the fortress of her house. Here in the city, she kept her windows closed, curtains drawn, doors locked; and whatever business she had with the world outside was transacted through a parted curtain over the open louvres next to her front door. He didn't know how she didn't suffocate inside that house. As soon as he got home from work his first task was to open the windows. As soon as he turned his back, she closed them.

To Beulah, the theft of George's bicycle pump (for she had not doubt that it was theft) was a signal that the criminals of the world were closing in on them, that somehow they had become people marked for further distress, and in that week whenever George went out on the porch to the rocking chair, she locked the front door. He had to knock to get back into the house.

George still held to the theory that someone had borrowed his pump, and that the culprit, not wanting to own up to the responsibility, had found it simpler to keep quiet. As he told Marcos, 'Not everybody have the courage to accept their wrong. A person do one wrong, a little, small inch of a wrong and they frighten to correct it, and that is what start them on the road to crime. But, believe me, Marcos, I wouldn't ask no question. I wouldn't vex, it will just be great if whoever borrow the pump, just bring it back and put it on the cycle. It will be real great.'

'George,' Marcos interrupted, for George was going on and on. 'I tell you already, nobody here aint borrow your bicycle pump.'

George, however, believed otherwise and he expected that any evening he would find the pump back in its place on the bicycle. After two weeks and no sign of the pump, George bought a new pump and fitted it on the bicycle. If he missed this one also, then he would know for sure that the first one was really stolen.

'You still leaving the pump on your bicycle,' Beulah said. 'You shame to walk with it in your hand? You shame to put it in your pocket?'

At the wedding of her niece the previous weekend, with relatives all around and everybody making nearly as much fuss over her as over the bride, she had put on a performance that convinced everybody that she and George were two love birds, and even after they returned to Port of Spain, she had continued to be civil to him. It was that peace that George found himself now straining to keep.

'Is fifteen years I parking my bicycle in the printery. I never walk with no pump. I lock the bicycle, yes; but I never walk with the pump.' He heard himself and was ashamed. He was whining.

'Well, you knows best. Leave it there for them to thief. You rich. You could afford to buy a new pump every week.'

George made for the porch. There on the old rocking chair, he watched the evening grow still and fussy and felt the heat

89

come up and watched the sun set, and he sat in the darkness, not bothering to turn on the lights, waiting to feel so sleepy that when he went into the furnace of a house, it would be to go directly to bed. He couldn't enter. Beulah had locked the front door. He began to bang the door. He was real angry. 'But, I right here. I right here, what you have to lock the door for?'

'George, you don't think I see you sleeping there on yourself in that rocking chair. You aint read where they tie up a woman inside her own house and thief all her jewellery. Her husband sleeping on the gallery, and the thief just waltz past him and tie her up and take her jewellery and leave him sleeping there. You didn't read it?'

'Well, is best I go and live in the jail.'

'I don't know about you,' said Beulah, 'but I prefer jail to the cemetery.'

George was really angry. He went back out on the porch, 'and leave the blasted door,' he said.

'Listen, man,' said Beulah, who could always give better than she got, 'Is not I who thief your bicycle pump. Don't take your vexation out on me.'

'Thief?' George tried to laugh. 'Who say anybody thief the pump?'

The next evening he went to get his bicycle, he found that the new pump, the one he had bought just a couple days before, was gone. For a moment, he stood in shock; then, the impulse came over him to steal somebody else's pump, anyone's. There were five bicycles parked in the lot. He went to the first one. There was no pump on it. He turned to the next. Not one of the bicycles had a pump. He felt his body grow chill and a space without bottom open up inside him and he was falling through it.

'I don't have a word to say,' Beulah said when she saw the pump was missing. 'Not a word.'

Out on the rocking chair, George began to wonder about the pumps. Who had removed them? Was it a thief? If it was, on what days did he make his rounds? Was he someone who set out to steal or did he just happen upon the pumps? Who it was that had removed the first pump? Was it the same person who had taken the second one? Was the first pump borrowed and the second one stolen? Or were both borrowed, or both stolen? I wonder, he thought, with a bit of pride, if he doesn't wonder what kind of fellar it is who leaving his pump on his bicycle? I wonder if he know that that fellar is me?

'And by the way, George.' Beulah was standing in the doorway, 'I take out some money from the bank today. We have to put in burglar proofing.'

'Tomorrow,' said George, 'I buying another pump.'

So he had bought another pump. This time, though, he set out to catch the thief, if thief it was. At odd moments he would jump up from his linotype machine and rush outside to the parking lot and his bicycle. At other times with an air of nonchalance, he would steal forth softly. He organised a variety of weapons to be at hand whenever he went into the parking lot. At one point he had hidden a stick, at another, an old hammer with a long piece of pipe iron as a handle. He put stones at definite points. He made a slingshot which he kept in the drawer of his desk. He drew diagrams detailing points from which he might approach the bicycle. He used his lunch hour to patrol the street in front the printery. He studied the passers-by. He noted all strangers who came into the printery. He questioned them. How suspicious everyone looked. Look at them, he thought, as he watched people go by in front the printery, one of them is the one who thief my bicycle pump.

For four weeks George kept up his surveillance. The slightest sound from outside would send him in a panic to investigate his bicycle. Fellars, noticing this pattern, began to bang things just to watch him jump. Workers started to become suspicious of him. Some thought that he was slacking, others, with more imagination, decided that he was smuggling something out of the printery, though what it was, they couldn't tell. Even Marcos became concerned.

'George,' Marcos said to him, your wife giving you trouble or what? Why you don't take a few days sick leave and rest yourself.'

91

At the end of the day he was exhausted. Home was no release, and he would sit on the rocking chair and watch the burglar proofing creeping around the house, making it, each day, into more of a prison. He had just begun to relax in the last few days; now, the bicycle pump was gone.

George unlocked the bicycle. He thought that he would be angry. Instead, there was a strange release, a kind of freedom, a peace. Then, rage surged in him, at the world, at the city, at Beulah, at the bicycle. And then he felt sorry for the bicycle and for the world and for Beulah and he thought of the thief. He tried to feel sorry for the thief, to feel superior to him; but, he didn't feel that feeling. He looked around at where he had hidden the stick and the hammer, and he saw the little heaps of stones that he had arranged so subtly as to blend into the lot, and it was for himself that he felt sorry.

George pushed his bicycle out of the lot, no longer hurrying to get to the football game, feeling that in his present state, if he went to the game, he would bring bad luck to his team. It was just a second division team, some young fellars from his part of Belmont, that he had been supporting for the last three years, but, so quietly, so shyly that although the crowds at their games were small and everyone seemed to know everyone else, no one knew him. The only time one of the players noticed him, to his surprise, was last season after they had lost a big game, a final, to John-John. He was making his way out of the Savannah when one of the players, going past him, put a hand on his shoulder and said, 'Hard game, uncle. Hard game!' and went on.

George walked, pushing the bicycle, all the way to the Savannah. At last he came to an empty bench below an overhanging samaan tree. He leaned his bicycle against the Savannah rails and went to the bench, but the scent of urine drove him back and with a sigh and a sense of adventure, he went a little way off and perched on the rails, took out his *Evening News* and began to read. From the corners of his eyes, he saw a young policeman approaching with easy, authoritative, rhythmic steps. Their eyes met, and something in their meeting made George feel a sense of guilt, in need of a defence. He turned back to his newspaper and waited for the policeman to go on. The policeman stopped. He looked at the bicycle. He looked at George. George looked up.

'Why you think they put benches there?' asked the policeman.

'Why they put benches ... ?' George didn't know what he was talking about.

'Those rails,' said the policeman. 'They have benches there for sitting down. That is why these rails always breaking down.'

George hopped off the rails. He felt stupid, guilty. He didn't know that he had been committing an offence. Look at that, eh? Harassing me for sitting down on the Savannah rails, and all over the place people thiefing, George thought as he went past a bench with a broken seat to one with the sun shining on it and sat down.

As soon as he began to read his *News*, a fellar came and plunked himself down next to him. He was barefooted, with no shirt under his grimy jacket. As soon as he sat down he put his face in his hands. 'Younger than me,' George thought. 'Mad, maybe.' All this from one glance, and he went back to his paper.

'Gimme one of your cigarettes.' The fellar's glaring eyes were fixed upon him.

'What you say?' An edge was in George's voice.

'I say, Chief, gimme one of your cigarettes, please.'

George was just going to say no when he realised that the fellar was pointing at the cigarette pack outlined in his breast pocket. George took out the pack, removed one cigarette and gave it to him.

'You have a light?' Not 'Chief' anymore, George thought.

George had a lighter, but he didn't want the fellar to touch it, so he lit the cigarette for him and watched him drag greedily on the cigarette, then blow out smoke with a great noise. George hated people to smoke like that. There was a young fellar in the printery who smoked in that greedy, noisy way.

93

Just for that, George never gave him a cigarette. George wanted to get up. He saw the fellar studying him. He hesitated. He didn't want his getting up to make the fellar feel offended.

'What is the headline?'

Relaxed, self-satisfied, smoke issuing from his nostrils, the fellar was looking at him. George held up the paper for him to see, but said, all the same, 'Thieves escape with three hundred dollars from El Socorro gas station.'

'Three hundred? Think the police will catch them?' his tone suddenly familiar.

'I dunno.'

'Most times the police does get tip off and they know just where to look.' With a kind of confidentiality, he added, 'They pay you for tipping off, you know.'

For no reason that he could think of, George said, 'You know they thief my bicycle pump today.'

The fellar grew alert, 'You have a mark on it?'

'A what?'

'A mark. You have a mark on it?'

'A mark? On a bicycle pump?'

'If you don't have a mark on it, then, it not yours, because, then, you see, you can't identify it. When you go and make a report to the police, you have to know what it is you loss, and how you will know if you don't have a mark on it? Whenever you buy a bicycle pump, always put a mark on it.'

To this piece of wisdom, George nodded.

'Everything I buy I have a mark on it.'

George nodded again. Faintly, from behind him, he could hear the roar of a crowd. 'Somebody score,' he said. He was wondering how his team was doing.

'Chief, you have a little change?' The fellar had on his face a confident, expectant look, as if he was asking for fees owed him for his legal advice.

George sized him up, feeling a kind of power, a kind of shame.

'Like they score another goal again,' the fellar said, smiling, his broken teeth coming into prominence, making him look guilty and smug.

94

But, George was looking at two fellars passing. One had a bicycle pump tucked in at his waist, between his belt.

'Chief, the change,' the fellar said.

George stood up and put a hand into his pocket and came upon the dinner mints he had bought from Mary. To give the dinner mints would, he felt, suggest too great a familiarity, as if they were friends. He felt for the coins, the change from the dollar bill, and he extracted every cent of it from his pocket and he put it all into the fellar's hand, coin by coin, the way Mary had given it to him. Then he went to his bicycle.

People had started to make their way home from the Savannah. George turned his bicycle towards Belmont. At the traffic lights he joined a number of cyclists and pedestrians waiting for the green. And for a moment he felt himself alive, in the thick of things, with the young fellars talking about the game they had just seen, a boy eyeing a girl, mothers with small children, the roar of passing vehicles, cyclists waiting to sprint across the street. A few brave souls, finding the lights taking too long to change, had begun to walk across the road. The traffic stopped for them and the lights turned green and George crossed in the stream of people. He gave his bicycle a little push, then hopped onto the saddle. He took a dinner mint from his pocket and began to take off the paper in which it was wrapped. Beulah was right, you can't leave your bicycle pump on your bicycle. All those people with pumps in their hands and at their waists, all of them was right. He put the dinner mint in his mouth, crumpled the paper and put it in his pocket.

At home, Beulah unlocked the door for him.

'They thief my bicycle pump,' he said.

'You sure they thief it?'

He didn't respond to her irony. He didn't say anything.

'Buy another pump and leave it on your bicycle again,' she said, trying to draw him out. 'They will thief it again.'

'Let them thief it,' he said, as he heard the burglar proofing clang shut behind him, right then thinking that it was cheaper to pay for a bicycle pump than to see the end of the world.

FLEURS

In the middle of the morning the stickfight drums began calling out to stickmen all over Cascadoux, in a grand terrible voice, so that in the Roman Catholic church acolytes at the mass found themselves moving in step with its deeper rhythm, and the drowsing old men awakened suddenly, startled by a voice they couldn't quite pin down and for the rest of the mass continued to gaze vaguely about the church as if to locate whoever it was that was calling their names.

After mass the fellars who usually spent Sunday mornings underneath the almond tree, playing rummy or shooting dice, were gone; and except for Piko crumpled drunkenly on the ground in front of Loy's closed rumshop and Traveller pacing near the bus stop, his battered suitcase stuffed with old clothes and ancient newspapers, bound with tattered neckties and pieces of string, the Junction was deserted as villagers returned from church. Walking behind her last two children, Fleurs' wife could feel her dress rustle and she felt the drums throbbing male and insistent inside her, quickening her heartbeat, making her feel a lofty dizziness and a victorious female surrender that made her remember the first time Fleurs took her in his arms and she looked up and saw how tall he was. For a moment her mind went back to that time and that tall Fleurs years ago, and she slowed down to hold the memory better. But then, seeing her two children moving further and further from her, she quickened her step, deciding that it was better to leave that time behind her.

When she got home she saw Fleurs sitting on the back step, sharpening his cutlass, noting in the same eyesweep the heaps of grass and weeds about the yard, and she chuckled, saying to the children, 'I wonder what vaps hit your father that make him decide to choose today to cutlass the grass?' when suddenly it hit her. What Fleurs doing home, when down at Nathan shop drums was beating? 'Fleurs?' But seeing the way his back was set and feeling the weight of the silence surrounding him, she stifled her question, thinking softly to herself, I better stay out his way this morning. Making for the front instead of going through the back door as she had intended, calling out, 'Fleurs, we come back!' The grunt of his reply satisfied her that her assessment of his mood was correct.

He went on sharpening his cutlass, grating the three-cornered file smoothly along the edge of the blade, watching the blade's edge gleam with every sharpening, eroding stroke, watching the grated metal fall off in tiny flecks. He was thinking of the sharpening of the cutlass and how every stroke of the file that sharpened it eroded it, made it thinner. Usually when his cutlass was worn down from sharpening he would turn it into a knife. You could sharpen a cutlass down to a needle, down to nothing, he thought, plucking the edge of the blade with his thumb to test it for sharpness.

Satisfied with its sharpness, he moved into the yard; and, bending before the uncut grass, he drew back his arm and swept his lifted cutlass through the grass, his hand going around and around in long swinging arcs, the cutlass scything through the grass, the cut grass, swept up in the swing of the cutlass, flying around his head, making in the morning sunlight a dissolving halo of green cascading grass.

From down the hill he heard a shout and a greater blaze of drumming and he breathed in and out self-consciously to keep himself calm. Bango reach, he thought, pausing. Bango, champion stickfighter, *obeah* man who nobody could defeat. Yes, is Bango who reach, hearing the deepened hush after the great shout and a new blaze of drumming, feeling a chill in his bones and a great wave, like fear, flow through him, through his belly and his knees and his ankles, and in his mind seeing Bango, with his black hat and his grey jacket, the grey of the feathers of a chicken hawk, and with that bird's blood red eyes, stepping towards the *gayelle* with the shuffling gait of a dancer or a thief, his head moving from side to side and his two hands upraised, triumphant, as he gave his wide, gold-teeth grin and the crowd parted for him and the three women he always brought to the stickfights with him.

Behind him, shaking a *shac shac* and holding aloft his 'bad' stick – the one mounted with the Amerindian spirit would be the usual one – the priestess, black, smooth, her red headtie setting off her round face with its piercing eyes and high cheek bones. He tried to picture the other two. Last year, following her, with his other stick and a bottle of rum was an Indian girl with a cricket cap on, delicate, loose, with the scent of violation and surrender about her, walking with a jaunty gladness as if she was proud to be counted as one of Bango's women; then, a tall one, a *travaseau*, a mix up one, brown, smooth, slatternly, with careless languorous movements and a face without shame, one eye black and blue where Bango had recently cuffed her: this one, looking into every stickman's eyes as she swept long loose and sullen to the front of the *gayelle*, as if she had come to seek a hero and was parading herself as the prize, but the stickmen were afraid to look at her lest she stir them to the craziness it was to tackle Bango.

They wouldn't miss me yet, he thought. They would be watching Bango, with his women taking off his jacket and his Shango priestess woman spinning around and making a libation with the white rum before giving him the bottle to take a drink. Now with the rum in his belly he and his women would begin his chant and he would go into the ring with his own terrible leaping dance, slow and fast and tall, and out of his terrible blood-red eyes he would take all in in the full ocean of his gaze, feeling their weight, their lightness, seeing the envy in their eyes, their fear, searching for the something that was missing among them. Let him look, Fleurs thought.

Fleurs' wife heard the noise from her kitchen, and she looked out and saw the grass flying to the sound of Fleurs' cutlassing, and she rattled the pots and pans, making a noise, hoping for his attention. But he didn't look in her direction. She had changed into home clothes and she called loudly to one of the children, so that Fleurs would hear, 'Go and ask your father if he want something to eat.'

The child came back saying, 'Pa don't want nothing.'

Still loudly, for Fleurs to hear, she said, 'What happen to your father? When I don't cook he does quarrel, when I cook he not eating.'

She went outside then, appeared before him with her moon face and her head tied with an old cotton dress, about her a kind of softness, the newness which she had come with from mass: 'What happen? You don't want nothing to eat? Whole morning you aint eat nothing, you know!'

He looked at her sideways, 'Watch yourself there,' making a step backwards, flicking his cutlass expertly at the grass, 'I aint hungry.'

She stood her ground, 'Fleurs, why you don't go and fight Bango? That is what you want to do, not so? Why you don't go?'

He glanced at her through the corners of his eyes; 'I want to fight Bango?'

'And that is what you do every year for the fifteen years I know you.'

'Well, I finish now. I done. Everybody in Cascadoux make friends with Bango, what I fighting Bango for? Aint you yourself say that?'

'I say that?'

'Yes. You say that.' He paused, looking at her and seeing the hurt in her eyes, 'But is true. Is just that you say it. It don't matter who say it. Is true. All the stickmen make friends with Bango.'

'How I could say everybody makes friends with Bango? Mr Joseph aint make friends with Bango.'

'Mr Joseph is a old man. Mr Joseph can't fight Bango. He could talk, yes; but Mr Joseph can't fight Bango.'

'I didn't mean it so. I didn't mean that it don't have nobody at all. It still have fellars who does fight Bango. Ancil and Calloway and Johnny and the one they call Beast: they does fight Bango.'

'Ancil and Calloway and Johnny and Beast? Bango does fart on them.'

'What you getting vex for?'

'A set of impressionists, that is what they is: just giving a impression. They don't really want to fight. They want to make style. They want to look pretty.'

'And that is not what I saying, Fleurs? Is not the same thing I saying: they creating an impression and you killing yourself in the ring.'

'And you want me to go?' He began to cutlass again.

'Anyhow,' she said, 'They will send and call you. They will send Phipps to call you.'

'Phipps? Let Phipps come.'

'They will send Phipps to call you, Fleurs. And Phipps will come and call you and you will go.'

'I will go?'

She tried to put a smile on her face, 'You will go, Fleurs. Phipps will come up the hill with his big fat self, blowing, shouting loud loud, "Hold the dogs before they bite me. With this sugar in my blood, I can't take a dog bite, you know." He will say, "Fleurs, man, what the hell happen with you? Man, what the arse you think you doing? You don't hear the drums? You don't know that you is the onliest man in Cascadoux to fight Bango?" He will come and make a big joke with you and give you a lotta talk and you will search your head and all your vexation will leave you, and you will go. You will go!'

'I will go?'

'Is fifteen years you doing it, Fleurs. People don't stop doing what they doing so long just so.'

'I will say, "Phipps, you see me here. I is a man with five children, and they have to eat. And I have a wife and she have to eat, and my yard. Look how tall the grass grow up in my yard. And is fifteen years I fighting Bango. Fifteen years for what? All the other stickmen make friends with Bango. What I fighting Bango for?"'

'"For the village," he will tell you. "For Cascadoux. For pride."'

100

'You know,' he said softly, 'In a way I wish I coulda make friends with Bango. I would make friends with Bango, not because I 'fraid Bango but because Bango is...Bango is true....'

'What you mean Bango is true? You don't know about all the wickedness Bango do, people land he take, people wife....'

'Because Bango is true to Bango. Because with all his tricks and his wickedness and his boasting and all the things I don't like him for, when you in the ring with Bango, you know he coming to kill you and you have to really battle.'

'And that is why you have to fight him, Phipps will tell you.'

'Not this time, though. No.'

'No?'

Later, from the kitchen, Fleurs' wife heard above the sound of Fleurs' cutlassing a new blaze of drumming, and she felt a strange anxiety, a kind of fear as when sometimes she alone and hear a car brakes screech and know her children playing near the road. She had her ears cocked, listening for the dogs to bark, expecting Phipps or one of them to come and call Fleurs. When Phipps came she would give him a good piece of her mind. The onliest time they prepared to come up this hill is when they want Fleurs to do something for them. Let him come.

She heard the drumbeat and the noise and shouting as she went about her chores; but, she didn't hear the dogs bark. After a while she didn't hear the sound of Fleurs' cutlass. She figured that he was on the back steps giving the blade a new edge; but when she looked outside she saw him at the place underneath the spouting where they caught water, at the barrel bathing. The children were playing cricket over in the little abandoned place where their neighbours had once lived.

Fleurs came into the kitchen. He had changed his clothes and she saw that he had his stick with him. With great effort she held her question. He looked a little sad, but fresher, and the terrible silence of earlier in the morning did not surround him.

With her ears straining for the bark of the dogs, she spoke, 'So where you going?'

'I going to meet Bango.'

'Yes,' she said, 'Is better you make friends with him. At least he will respect you.'

He smiled, 'I not going to make friends with Bango.'

'Lord!' she said, with a kind of anger, 'I don't know why you worrying with Cascadoux for.'

'Is not for Cascadoux I doing this for,' he said.

'Is not for Cascadoux?' She was looking into his eyes and seeing in them the truth, the earnestness, the fire and softness that had made her decide fifteen years ago that he was the man she wanted to struggle with and struggle for. She touched his arm, 'You know whole day you aint eat nothing.'

He relaxed a little then, 'You know I don't like to eat on this day.'

She went to the door with him. The children had stopped their game to watch him. And she watched him walk down the hill, a little taller than he had been earlier in the morning, but not quite as tall as that time long ago.

She still kinda hoped Phipps or somebody would come before he disappeared down the hill. She really wished one of them would come. Phipps and them was a set of dogs. She – Oh God! – really wished Phipps would come. But, how many things she wished for in her life ever happen?

When Fleurs reached the stickfight *gayelle*, he saw the crowd and felt the excitement, but he didn't quicken his step. In front of the rumshop in the open, where everybody could see him, Calloway stood running his fingers down the length of his stick. Three different coloured handkerchiefs were tied around his forehead, and a set of black and red beads hung from his neck. Fleurs didn't see Johnny or Beast; but, across the road lounged Ancil, with his baby face and his long fingernails, his brightly coloured shirt open and all his chest outside. At an angle from him, holding one of his hands, stood his woman, Mary, old enough for people to take the baby faced Ancil for her son, with rimless spectacles, stockings and a dress out of which her bottom jutted proudly.

Seeing Fleurs, Ancil called out, 'Fleurs, tell this woman please to let go my hand.'

'No,' Mary said. 'No. You not going in there to get kill. I not letting you go in no stickfighting ring.'

'You see my troubles,' Ancil moaned heroically.

Fleurs went on.

Bango was parading in the ring. Fleurs didn't say anything. He went straight through the crowd to the inside of the *gayelle*. No shout went up at his entry. Nobody didn't even notice that he was only now coming in; but, when he put his foot into the ring, the golden grin on Bango's face widened and the muscles on Bango's arms hardened as Bango took from his woman, the priestess, the *poui* stick mounted with the Amerindian spirit, and in his eyes shone that gleam that now, yes, there would be battle. And that was the reason why, listening up the hill, Fleurs's wife heard the terrible silence settle and the drums blaze forth again but with such an ordinariness that made her feel, with a new awakening pain, 'Oh God, they was expecting him all the time.'

THE MIDNIGHT ROBBER

Ash Wednesday morning. Carnival done. Who not stale drunk, still groggy. Hartley and Dan, in the carpenter-shed, idly thiefing a five, heard the sound of approaching boots. Dan leaped off the workbench and dived to the cupboard, pretending to be looking for nails, saying, 'Nail! Nails! I wonder where the nails?' Hartley, with a greater show of reluctance, his mouth shaped to *steups*, grabbed a jackplane and began to turn the levelling screw.

The man who came in was a squat, powerful fellar all in khaki. He had a sailor cap on his head and a hammer in his back pocket. Hartley let out the *steups*. Dan sprung from the cupboard and wagged a finger in the newcomer's face, 'King, why the hell you have to walk like the foreman for?'

Grinning, his cheeks bunching, sinking his eyes, bringing his spaced front teeth into prominence, the man addressed as King said, 'This is the boots I have. If you don't want me to walk like the foreman, why you don't buy a new pair for me?' In another tone, he asked, 'You see Jobe?'

'You always doing this stupidness,' Dan fretted, hopping again onto the workbench, 'You is not the foreman; don't walk like him.'

'If you want Jobe, check with the painters,' Hartley said, still turning the levelling screw of the jackplane.

'He not there,' King said.

'Try the office,' Dan said. 'It have a new typist-girl working there. Jobe always chatting her up.'

'The office is where I just come from.' King straightened his trousers, gripping his belt with two hands and heaving it around, 'Sombody should talk to Jobe, you know. I don't know why he wouldn't decide to pay the courts the money he owe them. Somebody should really talk to him.'

'He aint pay that money yet?' Dan looked at Hartley for confirmation.

'More than six months now,' King said. 'Always dodging from the police. Always hiding. And not to say he don't handle money. The boy working, he getting pay. Why all you don't talk to him?'

'Jobe is not paying that money.' Hartley's voice, usually slow and quavering, was firm. 'Jobe not paying one cent.' He rested down the jackplane.

'Not paying? Well, he going to go to jail this time,' King said. 'Police outside looking for him right now.'

'Jobe prepare to go to jail,' Hartley said. 'He not paying one cent of money to that woman.'

'But the woman is his married wife,' King said. 'She have rights. That is why people does get married in a legal way: to protect their rights.'

'The law too damn unfair,' Dan said, feeling in his pocket for a pack of cigarettes which he knew wasn't there, and looking at King's shirt pocket where a pack was outlined. Without taking out the pack, King reached into his pocket, drew out a single cigarette and gave it to Dan. 'The law too unfair,' Dan said again, speaking with the unlit cigarette between his lips, feeling his pocket for matches and leaning his head towards King for a light. 'Why is the man alone always have to pay?' as King lit the cigarette. 'But,' said Dan, drawing in the smoke, 'If was me, I would pay the money. I would pay the money rather than be dodging and peeping from the police.'

'Why one of you don't talk to him?' King said. 'This thing is trouble.'

'I tell you, Jobe is not paying,' Hartley said, a bit sharply. 'You can't force him to pay. He was only waiting for Carnival so he could play his masquerade. That is why he was dodging and peeping. But now that Carnival done and he finish play his mas', Jobe ready for anything.'

'If was me, I know I would pay. I married the woman, and we separate and she go to the courts for me to maintain her, and the courts tell me to pay. I would pay,' Dan said.

'So he really play mas'. What masquerade he play?' King asked.

'He play a Midnight Robber,' Hartley said.

'That is the big, the expensive masquerade he say he was going to play. How he look?'

'Good,' Hartley said.

'I woulda really like to see him. And his speech? He give any speech?'

Dan said, 'King, you sure you from Trinidad? You don't know that on Carnival day all Robbers does give speech?'

'Oh yeah? I see fellars calling theyself Robber, just blow their whistle and point their pistol and ask you for the money ... You play mas', Hartley?' And as Hartley shook his head. 'I thought you say you was going to play this year?'

'Every year Hartley does threaten to play mas',' Dan said. 'Every year ... Hartley, you ever play mas' at all, in your life?'

'I never play. In my whole life I never play. Every year I really promise myself, "This year I will play. This year". But, you have to plan these things. And though I have a whole year, I wait and wait and I don't plan and then before you know it, Carnival come, and then it too late to play.'

'Hartley, why you don't tell King that is your wife who stopping you from playing?' Laughing, he said, 'Hartley don't have a wife, he have a boss. She stop beating you yet, Hartley?'

'You have to plan these things,' Hartley said. 'And I don't plan and then I go home. How I could go home and just so say, I playing mas'? You have to plan, and I never plan.'

After the little silence, King made a step towards the door, 'I going. If you see Jobe tell him a police outside looking for him.'

Dan yawned and stretched all in one motion, 'Well, Jobe going down to prison today. He will get a good rest; he always tired on the job. King', he said, halting King, 'leave a smoke with me.'

106

Hartley said, 'Jobe free. He brave. He don't care a damn thing. Let the police come.'

'Man, you smoking too strong,' King said, grudgingly taking out his pack of cigarettes to give one to Dan. Just then Jobe came through the doorway, moving with his bumping walk, one hand swinging freely at his side, the other deep in a side pocket. Seeing them all looking at him, he smiled almost shyly, showing two gold splices between his teeth.

'Man, I looking all about for you,' King said.

Jobe grinned. He looked very pleased with himself, as if he knew exactly what the world was planning and he was one step ahead. 'I was in the back,' he said.

King made a noise with his lips, 'Brrrrt! Too much roti for Carnival, eh?'

Suddenly Jobe's face lit up, and he looked really delighted to see King. 'Hey, you see me yesterday?'

'That is the big, expensive mas' you say you was playing? Robber?'

'Tell me a mas' better than Robber, sweeter than Robber! You see me?'

'I look for you. But, in Port of Spain you can't see everybody on Carnival day.'

'Well, if you didn't see me, don't talk. Hartley see me. Tell him, Hartley. Tell him how I look. Tell him about my costume. My hat is the palace where the Prince of Darkness live. My shoes is the golden throne with nine snakes and nine lions guarding it. My cape is the voice of thunder that issue from my notorious father who came across the Sahara to lay waste the land, to drink the Nile, to create deserts, to destroy the palaces and plunder the precious works of art of Timbuktu and Zimbabwe. Tell him.'

Said King, 'That is the kinda speech you make?'

'You want to hear more speech,' Jobe said, crouching into his Robber's pose. 'Stop! Drop your keys and bend your knees ... And call me your master ... .'

'He was looking good,' Hartley said.

'Good. I was better than good. The best. And when I give my speech, people circle me, children follow me all over town. The other Robbers bow down before me. And, talk about a good time. Rum, woman, fete. It was the greatest.'

'So you had a good time, eh,' King said, with his own smile, heaving up his trousers once more.

Jobe closed his eyes, 'A sweet time. Rum, woman, bacchanal. Man, every day should be Carnival.'

'And what about the money you have for the courts?' Dan asked amidst a cloud of cigarette smoke.

'Courts?' Jobe asked scornfully, 'Courts? All you don't know me or what? Dan, I telling you, they could take me right now, if they want me.'

Hartley's smile seemed to spring warmly from his insides, 'You see what I tell you?'

'Courts? Let them lock me up, man. Jail aint build to put bananas to ripe.'

'But, you working, man.' Dan said.

'I know I working. I know.'

'Anyhow,' King said, turning to leave. 'Somebody outside looking for you.'

'Who looking for me?'

'You frighten? And you say, police could take you anytime?'

'Frighten?' Jobe exclaimed, 'Frighten? Me? Man, I never give the police any trouble in my life and I don't intend to start now. Frighten? Look, if it wasn't for Carnival, I in jail right now.'

'Okay, big man,' King said, leaving. 'Okay.'

Jobe turned to the others, 'What the hell wrong with King? King feel I 'fraid police. I had a good time for Carnival, what so hard about spending a little time in Golden Grove prison? The sun not hotter there than it is anywhere else in the island. But, look at this. King think I 'fraid the police.' Without waiting for any comment from his fellows, he pushed his hand into his pocket and with the other swinging at his side went with his bumping walk through the door.

'That boy,' Hartley said, admiration in his voice, 'That blasted boy.'

'Well, we better go in the yard and see how the work coming before the real foreman start to turn beast,' Dan said.

As Dan and Hartley left the room, they nearly collided with Jobe who was rushing back into the workshed. 'Man, police out there in truth,' Jobe said. He had a big red handkerchief in his back pocket, but he was wiping his face with his two hands.

Dan said, 'Boy, I would pay that money if I was you. The law is the law. And you working. You could afford it.'

'What you hustling the man into?' Hartley said. 'The man ask you for any advice?'

'You want him to go to prison?' Dan asked Hartley.

'Why I should want him to go to prison? But, the man is a big man. The man standing up on a principle. The man know what he doing,' Hartley said.

'Anybody see a new handsaw that I had this morning?' Jobe asked, his voice toneless.

'You working boy,' Dan said. 'You getting a pay every week.'

'You had a saw?' Hartley asked.

Dan was smiling, 'Maybe you leave it out in the back? Or maybe it in the cupboard. You want help to look for it?'

'We better look for it,' Hartley said.

They went into the workshed and searched and they didn't see any saw.

'You sure you didn't leave it out in the back?' Dan asked, smiling all the time.

Hartley sucked his teeth in disgust, 'I going on the job,' he said, and left Jobe and Dan in the shed.

When Jobe and Dan went outside, the policeman, who had been standing near the main building, began to push his bicycle towards them. Dan saw in Jobe's eyes the wild idea of escape, of flight. Seeing Dan's smile, Jobe started to grin, pushed one hand into a pocket and with the other swinging at his side set off in his bumping rhythmic walk towards the policeman.

'I hear you looking for Agustus Jobe,' Jobe said to the constable, standing before him, rocking back on his heels, two hands in his pockets.

The policeman stopped pushing his bicycle. 'Yes,' he said. 'I have a warrant here for his arrest.'

'Well, I is Jobe,' Jobe said.

'Man, you have some money here for us for a long time. You owe us some money more than six months now. Why you don't pay it?'

'Boss, yesterday was Carnival, where I going to get money to pay?'

'Well, you know what that means,' the policeman said, 'I have to take you down.'

'Yes, I know. You have your job to do. But, just do me one favour,' Jobe said. 'I will walk. I don't want no policeman to put his hands on me. Don't hold me. My girlfriend over in the office is looking at us. If she see you holding me she might start to bawl. You know how those women is?'

'Okay. But, man,' said the constable, transferring the folder with the warrant to his other hand as he began to push the bicycle, 'You know you's a hell of a man. Why you don't pay the money? Look, I could give you a break. I could give you a hour or two to see if you could get the money, even a part, and you could make an agreement to pay the rest next pay day.'

'And what Jobe say?' Hartley asked, as he listened to Dan give the details of the conversation which from his own distance he couldn't have heard.

'Jobe? Jobe say, "Man, I tell you, yesterday was Carnival. Today I aint have a cent and my whole salary tie up in debts. I clean".'

'And the police? What the police say?'

'"Well, if is so you want it, let's go"; so they go. And the boy working, yes. The boy getting a pay every week,' Dan began, but seeing the glow of Hartley's admiring smile, he was terrified to say another word.

JOEBELL AND AMERICA

ONE

Joebell find that he seeing too much hell in Trinidad so he make up his mind to leave and go away. The place he find he should go is America, where everybody have a motor car and you could ski on snow and where it have seventy-five channels of colour television that never sign off and you could sit down and watch for days, all the boxing and wrestling and basketball, right there as it happening. Money is the one problem that keeping him in Cunaripo; but that year as Christmas was coming, luck hit Joebell in the gamble, and for three days straight he win out the wappie. After he give two good pardners a stake and hand his mother a raise and buy a watch for his girl, he still have nineteen hundred and seventy-five Trinidad and Tobago dollars that is his own. That was the time. If Joebell don't go to America now, he will never go again.

But, a couple years earlier, Joebell make prison for a wounding, and before that they had him up for resisting arrest and using obscene language. Joebell have a record; and for him to get a passport he must first get a letter from the police to say that he is of good character. All the bribe Joebell try to bribe, he can't get this letter from the police. He prepare to pay a thousand dollars for the letter; but the police pardner who he had working on the matter keep telling him to come back and come back and come back. But another pardner tell him that with the same

111

thousand dollars he could get a whole new American passport, with new name and everything. The only thing a little ticklish is Joebell will have to talk Yankee.

Joebell smile, because if is one gift he have it is to talk languages, not Spanish and French and Italian and such, but he could talk English and American and Grenadian and Jamaican; and of all of them the one he love best is American. If that is the only problem, well, Joebell in America already.

But it have another problem. The fellar who fixing up the passport business for him tell him straight, if he try to go direct from Trinidad to America with the US passport, he could get arrest at the Trinidad airport, so the pardner advise that the best thing to do is for Joebell to try to get in through Puerto Rico where they have all those Spanish people and where the immigration don't be so fussy. Matter fix. Joebell write another pardner who he went to school with and who in the States seven years, and tell him he coming over, to look out for him, he will ring him from Puerto Rico.

Up in Independence Recreation Club where we gamble, since Joebell win this big money, he is a hero. All the fellars is suddenly his friend, everybody calling out, 'Joebell! Joebell!' some asking his opinion and some giving him advice on how to gamble his money. But Joebell not in no hurry. He know just as how you could win fast playing wappie, so you could lose fast too; and, although he want to stay in the wappie room and hear how we talk up his gambling ability, he decide that the safer thing to do is to go and play poker where if he have to lose he could lose more slow and where if he lucky he could win a good raise too. Joebell don't really have to be in the gambling club at all. His money is his own; but Joebell have himself down as a hero, and to win and run away is not classy. Joebell have himself down as classy.

Fellars' eyes open big big that night when they see Joebell heading for the poker room, because in there it have Japan and Fisherman from Mayaro and Captain and Papoye and a fellar named Morgan who every Thursday does come up from Tunapuna with a paper bag full with money and a knife in his shoe. Every man in there could real play poker.

112

In wappie, luck is the master; but in poker skill is what make luck work for you. When day break that Friday morning, Joebell stagger out the poker room with his whole body wash down with perspiration, out five hundred of his good dollars. Friday night he come back with the money he had give his girl to keep. By eleven he was down three. Fellars get silent and all of us vex to see how money he wait so long to get he giving away so easy. But, Joebell was really to go America in truth. In the middle of the poker, he leave the game to pee. On his way back, he walk into the wappie room. If you see Joebell: the whole front of his shirt open and wiping sweat from all behind his head. 'Heat!' somebody laugh and say. On the table that time is two card: Jack and Trey. Albon and Ram was winning everybody. The both of them like Trey. They gobbling up all bets. Was a Friday night. Waterworks get pay, County Council get pay. It had men from Forestry. It had fellars from the Housing Project. Money high high on the table. Joebell favourite card is Jack.

Ram was a loser the night Joebell win big; now, Ram on top. 'Who against trey?' Ram say. He don't look at Joebell, but everybody know is Joebell he talking to. Out of all Joebell money, one thousand gone to pay for the false passport, and, already in the poker he lose eight. Joebell have himself down as a hero. A hero can't turn away. Everybody waiting to see. They talking, but, they waiting to see what Joebell will do. Joebell wipe his face, then wipe his chest, then he wring out the perspiration from the handkerchief, fold the kerchief and put it round his neck, and bam, just like that, like how you see in pictures when the star boy, quiet all the time, begin to make his move, Joebell crawl right up the wappie table, fellars clearing the way for him, and, everything, he empty out everything he had in his two pocket, and, lazy lazy, like he really is that star boy, he say, 'Jack for this money!'

Ram was waiting, 'Count it, Casa,' Ram say.

When they count the money was two hundred and thirteen dollars and some change. Joebell throw the change for a broken hustler, Ram match him. Bam! Bam! Bam! In three card, Jack play.

'Double!' Joebell say. 'For all,' which mean that Joebell betting that another Jack play before any Trey.

Ram put some, and Albon put the rest, they sure is robbery.

Whap! Whap! Whap! Jack play. 'Devine!' Joebell say. That night Joebell leave the club with fifteen hundred dollars. Fellars calling him The Gambler of Natchez.

When we see Joebell next, his beard shave off, his head cut in a GI trim, and he walking with a fast kinda shuffle, his body leaned forward and his hands in his pockets and he talking Yankee: 'How ya doin, Main! Hi-ya, Baby!' And then we don't see Joebell in Cunaripo.

'Joebell gone away,' his mother, Miss Myrtle say, 'Praise God!'

If they have to give a medal for patience in Cunaripo, Miss Myrtle believe that the medal is hers just from the trials and tribulations she undergo with Joebell. Since he leave school his best friend is Trouble and wherever Trouble is, right there is Joebell.

'I shoulda mind my child myself,' she complain. 'His grandmother spoil him too much, make him feel he is too much of a star, make him believe that the world too easy.'

'The world don't owe you anything, boy,' she tell him. 'Try to be decent, son,' she say. Is like a stick break in Joebell two ears, he don't hear a word she have to say. She talk to him. She ask his uncle Floyd to talk to him. She go by the priest in Mount St Benedict to say a novena for him. She say the ninety-first psalm for him. She go by a *obeah* woman in Moruga to see what really happening to him. The *obeah* woman tell her to bring him quick so she could give him a bath and a guard to keep off the evil spirit that somebody have lighting on him. Joebell fly up in one big vexation with his mother for enticing him to go to the *obeah* woman: 'Ma, what stupidness you trying to get me in? You know I don't believe in the negromancy business. What blight you want to fall on me now? That is why it so hard for me to win in gamble, you crossing up my luck.'

But Miss Myrtle pray and she pray and at last, praise God, the answer come, not as how she did want it – you can't get

114

everything the way you want it – but, praise God, Joebell gone away. And to those that close to her, she whisper, 'America!' for that is the destination Joebell give her.

But Joebell aint reach America yet. His girl Alicia, who working at Last Chance snackette on the Cunaripo road is the only one he tell that Puerto Rico is the place he trying to get to. Since she take up with Joebell, her mother quarrelling with her every day, 'How a nice girl like you could get in with such a vagabond fellar? You don't have eyes in your head to see that the boy is only trouble?' They talk to her, they tell her how he stab a man in the gambling club and went to jail. They tell her how he have this ugly beard on his face and this ugly look in his face. They tell her how he don't work nowhere regular, 'Child, why you bringing this cross into your life?' they ask her. They get her Uncle Matthew to talk to her. They carry her to Mount St Benedict for the priest to say a novena for her. They give her the ninety-first psalm to say. They carry her to Moruga to a *obeah* woman who bathe her in a tub with bush, and smoke incense all over her to untangle her mind from Joebell.

But there is a style about Joebell that she like. Is a dream in him that she see. And a sad craziness that make her sad too but in a happy kinda way. The first time she see him in the snackette, she watch him and don't say nothing but, she think, Hey! who he think he is? He come in the snackette with this foolish grin on his face and this strolling walk and this kinda commanding way about him and sit down at the table with his legs wide open, taking up a big space as if he spending a hundred dollars, and all he ask for is a coconut roll and a juice. And then he call her again, this time he want a napkin and a toothpick. Napkins and toothpicks is for people who eating food; but she give them to him. And still he sit down there with some blight, some trouble hanging over him, looking for somebody to quarrel with or for something to get him vex so he could parade. She just do her work, and not a word she tell him. And just like that, just so by himself he cool down and start talking to her though they didn't introduce.

Everything he talk about is big: big mountains and big cars and race horses and heavyweight boxing champions and people in America – everything big. And she look at him from behind the counter and she see his sad craziness and she hear him talk about all this bigness far away, that make her feel too that she would like to go somewhere and be somebody, and just like that, without any words, or touching it begin.

Sometimes he'd come in the snackette, walking big and singing, and those times he'd be so broke all he could afford to call for'd be a glass of cold water. He wanted to be a calypsonian, he say; but he didn't have no great tune and his compositions wasn't so great either and everything he sing had a kinda sadness about it, no matter how he sing it. Before they start talking direct to one another he'd sing, closing his eyes and hunching his shoulders, and people in the snackette'd think he was just making joke; but, she know the song was for her and she'd feel pretty and sad and think about places far away. He used to sing in a country and western style, this song: his own composition:

Gonna take ma baby
Away on a trip
Gonna take ma baby
Yip yip yip
We gonna travel far
To New Orleans
Me and ma baby
Be digging the scene

If somebody came in and had to be served, he'd stop singing while she served them, then he'd start up again. And just so, without saying anything or touching or anything, she was his girl.

She never tell him about the trouble she was getting at home because of him. In fact she hardly talk at all. She'd just sit there behind the counter and listen to him. He had another calypso that he thought would be a hit.

Look at Mahatma Ghandi
Look at Hitler and Mussolini
Look at Uriah Butler
Look at Kwame Nkrumah
Great as they was
Everyone of them had to stand the pressure

116

He used to take up the paper that was on one side of the counter and sit down and read it, 'Derby day,' he would say. 'Look at the horses running,' and he would read out the horses' names. Or it would be boxing, and he would say Muhammed boxing today, or Sugar. He talked about these people as if they were personal friends of his. One day he brought her five pounds of deer wrapped in a big brown paper bag. She was sure he pay a lot of money for it. 'Put this in the fridge until you going home.' Chenette, mangoes, oranges, sapodillas, he was always bringing things for her. When her mother ask her where she was getting these things, she tell her that the owner of the place give them to her. For her birthday Joebell bring her a big box wrapped in fancy paper and went away, so proud and shy, he couldn't stand to see her open it, and when she open it it was a vase with a whole bunch of flowers made from coloured feathers and a big birthday card with an inscription: From guess who?

'Now, who give you this? The owner?' her mother asked.

She had to make up another story.

When he was broke she would slip him a dollar or two of her own money and if he win in the gamble he would give her some of the money to keep for him, but she didn't keep it long, he mostly always came back for it next day. And they didn't have to say anything to understand each other. He would just watch her and she would know from his face if he was broke and want a dollar or if he just drop in to see her, and he could tell from her face if she want him to stay away altogether that day or if he should make a turn and come again or what. He didn't get to go no place with her, cause in the night when the snackette close her big brother would be waiting to take her home.

'Thank God!' her mother say when she hear Joebell gone away. 'Thank you, Master Jesus, for helping to deliver this child from the clutches of that vagabond.' She was so happy she hold a thanksgiving feast, buy sweet drinks and make cake and invite all the neighbour's little children; and she was surprise that Alicia was smiling. But Alicia was thinking, Lord, just please let him get to America, they will see who is vagabond. Lord, just let him get through that immigration they will see happiness when he send for me.

117

The fellars go round by the snackette where Alicia working and they ask for Joebell.

'Joebell gone away,' she tell them.

'Gone away and leave a nice girl like you? If was me I would never leave you.'

And she just smile that smile that make her look like she crying and she mumble something that don't mean nothing, but if you listen good is, 'Well, is not you.'

'Why you don't let me take you to the dance in the Centre Saturday? Joey Lewis playing. Why you don't come and forget that crazy fellar?'

But Alicia smile no, all the time thinking, wait until he send for me, you will see who crazy. And she sell the cake and the coconut roll and sweet drink and mauby that they ask for and take their money and give them their change and move off with that soft, bright, drowsy sadness that stir fellars, that make them sit down and drink their sweet drink and eat their coconut roll and look at her face with the spread of her nose and the lips stretch across her mouth in a full round soft curve and her far away eyes and think how lucky Joebell is.

When Joebell get the passport he look at the picture in it and he say, 'Wait! This fellar aint look like me. A blind man could see this is not me.'

'I know you woulda say that,' the pardner with the passport say, 'You could see you don't know nothing about the American immigration. Listen, in America, every black face is the same to white people. They don't see no difference. And this fellar here is the same height as you, roughly the same age. That is what you have to think about, those little details, not how his face looking.' That was his pardner talking.

'You saying this is me, this fellar here is me?' Joebell ask again. 'You want them to lock me up or what, man? This is what I pay a thousand dollars for? A lock up?'

'Look, you have no worry. I went America one time on a passport where the fellar had a beard and I was shave clean and they aint question me. If you was white you mighta have a problem, but black, man, you easy.'

118

And in truth when he think of it, Joebell could see the point, cause he aint sure he could tell the difference between two Chinese.

'But, wait!' Joebell say, 'Suppose I meet up a black immigration?'

'Ah!' the fellar say, 'You thinking. Anyhow, it aint have that many, but, if you see one stay far from him.'

So Joebell, with his passport in his pocket, get a fellar who running contraband to carry him to Venezuela where his brother was living. He decide to spend a couple days by his brother and from there take a plane to Puerto Rico, in transit to America.

His brother had a job as a motor car mechanic.

'Why you don't stay here?' his brother tell him, 'It have work here you could get. And TV does be on whole day.'

'The TV in Spanish,' Joebell tell him.

'You could learn Spanish.'

'By the time I finish learn Spanish I is a old man,' Joebell say, '*Caramba! Caramba! Habla! Habla!* No. And besides I done pay my thousand dollars. I have my American passport. I is an American citizen. And,' he whisper, softening just at the thought of her, 'I have a girl who coming to meet me in America.'

Joebell leave Venezuela in a brown suit that he get from his brother, a strong-looking pair of brown leather boots that he buy, with buckels instead of laces, a cowboy hat on his head and an old camera from his brother over his shoulder and in his mouth is a cigar, and now he is James Armstrong Brady of the one hundred and twenty-fifth infantry regiment from Alabama, Vietnam Veteran, twenty-six years old. And when he reach the airport in Puerto Rico he walk with a stagger and he puff his cigar like he already home in the United States of America. And not for one moment it don't strike Joebell that he doing any wrong.

No. Joebell believe the whole world is a hustle. He believe everybody running some game, putting on some show and the only thing that separate people is that some have power and others don't have none, that who in in and who out out, and that is exactly what Joebell kick against, because Joebell have himself down as a hero too and he not prepare to sit down timid timid as

119

if he stupid and see a set of bluffers take over the world, and he stay wasting away in Cunaripo; and that is Joebell's trouble. That is what people call his craziness, is that that mark him out. That is the 'light' that the *obeah* woman in Moruga see burning on him, is that that frighten his mother and charm Alicia and make her mother want to pry her loose from him. Is that that fellars see when they see him throw down his last hundred dollars on a single card, as if he know it going to play. The thing is that Joebell really don't be betting on the card, Joebell does be betting on himself. He don't be trying to guess about which card is the right one, he is trying to find that power in himself that will make him call correct. And that power is what Joebell searching for as he queue up in the line leading to the immigration entering Puerto Rico. Is that power that he calling up in himself as he stand there, because if he can feel that power, if that power come inside him, then, nothing could stop him. And now this was it.

'Mr Brady?' The immigration man look up from Joebell passport and say, same time turning the leaves of the passport. And he glance at Joebell and he look at the picture. And he take up another book and look in it, and look again at Joebell; and maybe it is that power Joebell reaching for, that thing inside him, his craziness that look like arrogance, that put a kinda sneer on his face that make the immigration fellar take another look.

'Vietnam Veteran? Mr Brady, where you coming from?'

'Venezuela.'

The fellar ask a few more questions. He is asking Joebell more questions than he ask anybody.

'Whatsamatta? Watsa problem?' Joebell ask, 'Man, I aint never seen such incompetency as you got here. This is boring. Hey, I've got a plane to catch. I aint got all day.'

All in the airport people looking at Joebell 'cause Joebell not talking easy, and he biting his cigar so that his words coming to the immigration through his teeth. Why Joebell get on so is because Joebell believe that one of the main marks of a real American is that he don't stand no nonsense. Any time you get a real American in an aggravating situation, the first thing he do is let his voice be heard in objection: in other words, he does get on.

120

In fact that is one of the things Joebell admire most about Americans: they like to get on. They don't care who hear them, they going to open their mouth and talk for their rights. So that is why Joebell get on so about incompetency and missing his plane and so on. Most fellars who didn't know what it was to be a real American woulda take it cool. Joebell know what he doing.

'Sir, please step into the first room on your right and take a seat until your name is called.' Now is the immigration talking, and the fellar firm and he not frighten, 'cause he is American too. I don't know if Joebell didn't realise that before he get on. That is the kind of miscalculation Joebell does make sometimes in gambling and in life.

'Maan, just you remember I gotta plane to catch,' and Joebell step off, with that slow, tall insolence like Jack Palance getting off his horse in *Shane*, but he take off his hat and go and sit down where the fellar tell him to sit down.

It had seven other people in the room but Joebell go and sit down alone by himself because with all the talk he talking big, Joebell just playing for time, just trying to put them off; and now he start figuring serious how he going to get through this one. And he feeling for that power, that craziness that sometimes take him over when he in a wappie game, when every bet he call he call right; and he telling himself they can't trap him with any question because he grow up in America right there in Trinidad. In his grandmother days was the British; but he know from Al Jolson to James Brown. He know Tallahashie bridge and Rocktow mountain. He know Doris Day and Frank Sinatra. He know America. And Joebell settle himself down not bothering to remember anything, just calling up his power. And then he see this tall black fellar over six foot five enter the room. At a glance Joebell could tell he's a crook, and next thing he know is this fellar coming to sit down side of him.

TWO

I sit down there by myself alone and I know they watching me. Everybody else in the room white. This black fellar come in the

121

room, with beads of perspiration running down his face and his eyes wild and he looking round like he escape. As soon as I see him I say 'Oh God!' because I know with all the empty seats all about the place is me he coming to. He don't know my troubles. He believe I want friends. I want to tell him 'Listen, man, I love you. I really dig my people, but now is not the time to come and talk to me. Go and be friendly by those other people, they could afford to be friends with you.' But I can't tell him that 'cause I don't want to offend him and I have to watch how I talking in case in my situation I slip from American to Trinidadian. He shake my hand in the Black Power sign. And we sit down there side by side, two crooks, he and me, unless he's a spy they send to spy on me.

I letting him do all the talking, I just nodding and saying yeah, yeah.

He's an American who just come out of jail in Puerto Rico for dope or something. He was in Vietnam too. He talking, but I really aint listening to him. I thinking how my plane going. I thinking about Alicia and how sad her face will get when she don't get the letter that I suppose to send for her to come to America. I thinking about my mother and about the fellars up in Independence Recreation Club and around the wappie table when the betting slow, how they will talk about me, 'Natchez', who win in the wappie and go to America – nobody ever do that before – and I thinking how nice it will be for me and Alicia after we spend some time in America to go back home to Trinidad for a holiday and stay in the Hilton and hire a big car and go to see her mother. I think about the Spanish I woulda have to learn if I did stay in Venezuela.

At last they call me inside another room. This time I go cool. It have two fellars in this room, a big tough one with a stone face and a jaw like a steel trap, and a small brisk one with eyes like a squirrel. The small one is smoking a cigarette. The tough one is the one asking questions. The small one just sit down there with his squirrel eyes watching me, and smoking his cigarette.

'What's your name?'

And I watching his jaw how they clamping down on the words. 'Ma name is James Armstrong Brady.'

'Age?'

And he go through a whole long set of questions.

'You're a Vietnam Veteran, you say? Where did you train?'

And I smile 'cause I see enough war pictures to know, 'Nor' Carolina,' I say.

'Went to school there?'

I tell him where I went to school. He ask questions until I dizzy.

The both of them know I lying, and maybe they coulda just throw me in jail just so without no big interrogation; but, America. That is why I love America. They love a challenge. Something in my style is a challenge to them, and they just don't want to lock me up because they have the power, they want to trap me plain for even me to see. So now is me, Joebell, and these two Yankees. And I waiting, 'cause I grow up on John Wayne and Gary Cooper and Audie Murphy and James Stewart and Jeff Chandler. I know the Dodgers and Phillies, the Redskins and the Dallas Cowboys, Green Bay Packers and the Vikings. I know Walt Frazier and Doctor J, and Bill Russell and Wilt Chamberlain. Really, in truth, I know America so much, I feel American. Is just that I aint born there.

As fast as the squirrel-eye one finish smoke one cigarette, he light another one. He aint saying nothing, only listening. At last he put out his cigarette, he say, 'Recite the alphabet.'

'Say what?'

'The alphabet. Recite it.'

And just so I know I get catch. The question too easy. Too easy like a calm blue sea. And, pardner, I look at that sea and I think about Alicia and the warm soft curving sadness of her lips and her eyes full with crying, make me feel to cry for me and Alicia and Trinidad and America and I know like when you make a bet you see a certain card play that it will be a miracle if the card you bet on play. I lose, I know. But I is still a hero. I can't bluff forever. I have myself down as classy. And, really, I wasn't frighten for nothing, not for nothing, wasn't afraid of jail or of poverty or of Puerto Rico or America and I wasn't vex with the fellar who sell me the passport for the thousand dollars, nor with

123

Iron Jaw and Squirrel Eyes. In fact, I kinda respect them. 'A ... B ... C ...' And Squirrel Eyes take out another cigarette and don't light it, just keep knocking it against the pack, Tock! Tock! Tock! K ... L ... M ... And I feel I love Alicia ... V ... W ... and I hear Paul Robeson sing 'Old Man River' and I see Sammy Davis Junior dance Mr Bojangle's dance and I hear Nina Simone humming humming 'Suzanne', and I love Alicia; and I hear Harry Belafonte's rasping call, 'Daay-o, Daaay-o! Daylight come and me want to go home,' and Aretha Franklyn screaming screaming, ' ... Y ... Zed.'

'Bastard!' the squirrel eyes cry out, 'Got you!'

And straightaway from another door two police weighed down with all their keys and their handcuffs and their pistols and their night stick and torch light enter and clink their handcuffs on my hands. They catch me. God! And now, how to go? I think about getting on like an American, but I never see an American lose. I think about making a performance like the British, steady, stiff upper lip like Alec Guinness in *The Bridge over the River Kwai*, but with my hat and my boots and my piece of cigar, that didn't match, so I say I might as well take my losses like a West Indian, like a Trinidadian. I decide to sing. It was the classiest thing that ever pass through Puerto Rico airport, me with these handcuffs on, walking between these two police and singing,

Gonna take ma baby
Away on a trip
Gonna take ma baby
Yip yip yip
We gonna travel far
To New Orleans
Me and ma Baby
Be digging the scene

SHOEMAKER ARNOLD

Shoemaker Arnold stood at the doorway of his little shoemaker shop, hands on hips, his body stiffened in that proprietorial and undefeated stubbornness, announcing, not without some satisfaction, that if in his life he had not been triumphant, neither had the world defeated him. It would be hard, though, to imagine how he could be defeated, since he exuded such a hard tough unrelenting cantankerousness, gave off such a sense of readiness for confrontation, that if Trouble had to pick someone to clash with, Shoemaker Arnold would not be the one. To him, the world was his shoemaker shop. There he was master and anyone entering would have to surrender not only to his opinion on shoes and leather and shoemaker apprentices, but to his views on politics, women, religion, flying objects, or any of the myriad subjects he decided to discourse upon, so that over the years he had arrived at a position where none of the villagers bothered to dispute him, and to any who dared maintain a view contrary to the one he was affirming, he was quick to point out, 'This place is mine. Here, I do as I please. I say what I want. Who don't like it, the door is open.'

His wife had herself taken that advice many years earlier, and had moved not only out of his house but out of the village, taking with her their three children, leaving him with his opinions, an increasing taste for alcohol, and the tedium of having to prepare his own meals. It is possible that he would have liked to take one of the village girls to live with him, but he was too proud to accept that he had even that need, and he would look at the girls go by outside his shop, hiding, behind his dissatisfied scowl a fine, appraising, if not lecherous, eye; but if one of them happened to look in, he would snarl at her, 'What you want here?' So that between him and the village girls there existed this teasing challenging relationship of antagonism and desire, the girls themselves walking with greater flourish and style when they went past his shoemaker shop, swinging their backsides and cutting their eyes, and he, scowling, dissatisfied.

With the young men of the village his relationship was no better. As far as he was concerned none of them wanted to work and he had no intention of letting them use his shoemaker shop as a place to loiter. Over the years he had taken on numerous apprentices, keeping them for a month or two and sometimes for just a single day, then getting rid of them; and it was not until Norbert came to work with him that he had had what could be considered regular help.

Norbert, however, was no boy. He was a drifter, a rum drinker, and exactly that sort of person that one did not expect Arnold to tolerate for more than five minutes. Norbert teased the girls, was chummy with the loiterers, gambled, drank too much, and, anytime the spirit moved him, would up and take off and not return for as much as a month. Arnold always accepted him back. Of course he quarrelled, he complained, but the villagers who heard him were firm in their reply: 'Man, you like it. You like Norbert going and coming when he please, doing what he want. You like it.'

More than his leavings, Norbert would steal Arnold's money, sell a pair of shoes, lose a side of shoes, charge people and pocket the money, not charge some people at all, and do every other form of wickedness to be imagined in the circumstances. It must have been that because Norbert was so indisputably in the wrong that it moved Arnold to exhibit one of his rare qualities, compassion. It was as if Arnold needed Norbert as the means through which to declare not only to the world, but to declare to himself, that he had such a quality; to prove to himself that he was not the cantankerous person people made him out to be. So, on those occasions when he welcomed back the everlasting prodigal, Arnold, forgiving and compassionate, would be imbued with the idea of his own goodness, and he would feel that in the world, truly, there was not a more generous soul than he.

Today was one such day. Two weeks before Christmas, Norbert had left to go for a piece of ice over by the rumshop a few yards away. He had returned the day before. 'Yes,' thought Arnold, 'look at me, I not vex.' Arnold was glad for the help, for he had work that people had already paid advances on and would be coming in to collect before New Year's day. That was one thing he appreciated about Norbert. Norbert was faithful, but Norbert had to get serious about the right things. He was faithful to too many frivolous things. He was faithful to the girl who dropped in and wanted a dress, to a friend who wanted a nip. A friend would pass in a truck and say, 'Norbert, we going San Fernando.' Norbert would put down the shoes he was repairing, jump on the truck without a change of underwear even, and go. It wasn't rum. It was some craziness, something inside him that just took hold of him. Sometimes, a week later he would return, grimy, stale, thin, as if he had just hitch-hiked around the world in a coal bin, slip into the shop, sit down and go back to work as if nothing out of the way had happened. And he could work when he was working. Norbert could work. Any shop in Port of Spain would be glad to have him. Faithful worker. Look at that! This week when most tradesmen had already closed up for Christmas there was Norbert working like a machine to get people's shoes ready. Appreciation. It shows appreciation. People don't have appreciation again, but Norbert had appreciation. Is how you treat people, he thought. You have to understand them. Look how cool he here working in my shoemaker shop this big Old Year's day when all over the island people feteing.

At the door he was watching two girls going down the street, nice, young, with the spirit of rain and breezes about them. Then his eyes picked up a donkey cart approaching slowly from the direction of the Main Road which led to Sangre Grande, and he stood there in front his shoemaker shop, his lips pulled back and looked at the cart come up and go past. Old Man Moses, the charcoal burner, sat dozing in the front, his chin on his chest, and the reins in his lap. To the back sat a small boy with a cap on and a ragged shirt, his eyes alert, his feet hanging over the sides of the cart, one hand resting on a small brown and white dog sitting next to him.

Place dead, he thought, seeing the girls returning; and, looking up at the sky, he saw the dark clouds and that it was going to rain and he looked at the cart. 'Moses going up in the bush. Rain going to soak his tail,' he said. And as if suddenly irritated by that thought, he said, 'You mean Moses aint have no family he could spend New Year's by,' his tone drumming up his outrage. 'Why his family can't take him in and let him eat and drink and be merry for the New Year instead of going up in the bush for rain to soak his tail? That is how we living in this world,' he said, seating himself on the workbench and reaching for the shoe to be repaired. 'That is how we living. Like beast.'

'Maybe he want to go up in the bush,' Norbert said. 'Maybe he going to attend his coal pit, to watch it that the coals don't burn up and turn powder.'

'Like blasted beast,' Arnold said. 'Beast,' as if he had not heard Norbert.

But afterwards, after he had begun to work, had gotten into the rhythm of sewing and cutting and pounding leather, and had begun the soft firm waxing of the twine, the sense of the approaching New Year hit him and he thought of the girls and the rain, and he thought of his own life and his loneliness and his drinking and of the world and of people, people without families, on pavements and in orphanages and those on park benches below trees. 'The world have to check up on itself,' he said. 'The world have to check up … . And you, Norbert, you have to check up on yourself,' he said broaching for the first time the matter of Norbert's leaving two weeks before Christmas and returning only yesterday. 'I not against you. You know I not against you. I talk because I know what life is. I talk because I know about time. Time is all we have, boy. Time … . A Time to live and a time to die. You hear what I say. Norbert?'

128

'What you say?'

'I say, it have a time to live and a time to die ... . You think we living?'

Norbert leaned his head back a little, and for a few moments he seemed to be gazing into space, thinking, concentrating.

'We dying,' he said, 'we dying no arse.'

'You damn right. Rum killing us. Rum. Not bombs or Cancer or something sensible. Rum. You feel rum should kill you?'

Norbert drew the twine out of the stitch and smiled.

'But in this place, rum must kill you. What else here could kill a man? What else to do but drink and waste and die. That is why I talk. People don't understand me when I talk; but that is why I talk.'

Norbert threaded the twine through the stitch with his smile and in one hand he held the shoe and with the other he drew out the twine: 'We dying no arse!' as if he had hit on some truth to be treasured now. 'We dying ... no arse.'

'That is why I talk. I want us ... you to check up, to put a little oil in your lamp, to put a little water in your wine.'

Norbert laughed. He was thinking with glee, even as he said it, 'We dying no arse, all o'we, everybody. Ha ha ha ha,' and he took up his hammer and started to pound in the leather over the stitch 'Ha ha ha ha ha!'

Arnold had finished the shoe he was repairing and he saw now the pile of shoes in the shoemaker shop. 'One day I going to sell out all the shoes that people leave here. They hurry hurry for you to repair them. You use leather, twine, nails, time. You use time, and a year later, the shoes still here watching you. Going to sell out every blasted one of them this New Year.'

'All o'we, every one of us,' Norbert chimed.

'That is why this shoemaker shop always like a junk heap.'

'Let us send for a nip of rum, nuh,' Norbert said, and as Arnold looked at him, 'I will buy. This is Old Year's, man.'

'Rum?' Arnold paused. 'How old you is, boy?'

'Twenty-nine.'

'Twenty-nine! You making joke. You mean I twenty-one years older than you? We dying in truth. Norbert, we dying. Boy, life

129

really mash you up.' And he threw down the shoe he was going to repair.

'We have three more shoes that people coming for this evening,' Norbert said, cautioning. 'Corbie shoes, Synto shoes and Willie Paul sandals.'

Arnold leaned and picked up the shoe again. 'Life aint treat you good at all. I is twenty-one years older than you? Norbert, you have to check up,' he said. 'Listen, man, you getting me frighten. When I see young fellars like you in this condition I does get frighten … . Listen. Norbert, tell me something! I looking mash up like you? Eh? Tell me the truth. I looking mash up like you?'

Norbert said, 'We dying no arse, all o'we everybody.'

'No. Serious. Tell me, I looking mash up like you?'

'Look, somebody by the door,' Norbert said.

'What you want?' Arnold snapped. It was one of the village girls, a plump one with a bit of her hair plastered down over her forehead making her look like a fat pony.

'You don't have to shout at me, you know. I come for Synto shoes.'

'Well, I don't want no loitering by the door. Come inside and siddown and wait. I now finishing it.' He saw her turn to look outside and she said something to sombody. 'Somebody there with you?'

'She don't want to come in.'

'Let her come in too. I don't want no loitering by the door. This is a business place.' He called out, 'Come in. What you hanging back for?'

The girl who came in was the one that reminded him of rain and moss and leaves. He tried to look away from her, but he couldn't. And she too was looking at him.

'You 'fraid me?' And he didn't know how his voice sounded, though at that moment he thought he wanted it to sound tough.

'A little,' she said.

'Siddown,' he said, and Norbert's eyes nearly popped open. What was he seeing? Arnold was getting up and taking the chair from the corner, dusting it too. 'Sit down. The shoes will finish just now.'

130

She watched him work on the shoe and the whole shoemaker shop was big like all space and filled with breathlessness and rain and moss and green leaves.

'You is Synto daughter?'

'Niece,' she said.

And when he was finished repairing the shoes, he looked around for a paper bag in which to put them, because he saw that she had not come with any bag herself. 'When you coming for shoes you must bring something to wrap it in. You can't go about with shoes in your hand just so.'

'Yes,' she said. 'Yes.' Quickly as if wanting to please him.

He found some old newspaper he was saving to read when he had time and he folded the shoes in it and wrapped it with twine and he gave it to her and she took it and she said 'thank you' with that funny little face and that voice that made something inside him ache and she left, leaving the breathlessness in the shoemaker shop and the scent of moss and aloes and leaves and it was like if all his work was finished. And when he caught his breath he pushed his hand in his pocket and brought out money and said to Norbert, 'Go and buy a nip.' And they drank the nip, the two of them, and he asked Norbert, 'Where you went when you went for the ice?' And he wasn't really listening for no answer, for he had just then understood how Norbert could, how a man could, leave and go off. He had just understood how he could leave everything and go just so.

'You had a good time?' Though those weren't the right words. A good time! People didn't leave for a good time. It was for something more. It was out of something deeper, a call, something that was awakened in the blood, the mind. 'You know what I mean?'

'Yes,' Norbert said, kinda sadly, soft, and frightened for Arnold but not wanting to show it.

Arnold said, 'I dying too.' And then he stood up and said sort of sudden, 'This place need some pictures. And we must keep paper bags like in a real "establishment",' and with that same smile he said, 'Look at that, eh. That girl say she 'fraid me a little. Yes, I suppose that is correct. A little. Not that she 'fraid me. She

131

'fraid me a little.'

When they closed the shop that evening they both went up Tapana Trace by Britto. Britto was waiting for them.

'Ah,' he said, 'Man reach. Since before Christmas I drinking and I can't get drunk. It aint have man to drink rum with again. But I see man now.'

They went inside and Britto cleared the table and put three bottles of rum on it, one before each one of them, a mug of water and a glass each, and they began to drink.

Half an hour later the *parang* band came in and they sang an *aguanaldo* and a *joropo* and they drank and Norbert started to sing with them the nice festive Spanish music that made Arnold wish he could cry. And then it was night and the *parang* band was still there and Britto wife family came in and a couple of Britto friends and the women started dancing with the little children and then Josephine, Britto neighbour, held on to Arnold and pulled him onto the floor to dance, and he tried to dance a little and then he sat down and they took down the gas lamp and pumped it and Britto's wife brought out the portion of *lappe* that she had been cooking on a wood fire in the yard and they ate and drank and with the music and the children and the women, everything, the whole thing was real sweet. It was real sweet. And Norbert, more drunk than sober, sitting in a corner chatting down Clemencia sister picked up another bottle of rum, broke the seal and about to put it to his lips, caught Arnold's eye and hesitated, then he put it to his lips again. He said, 'Let me dead.' And Arnold sat and thought about this girl, the one that filled the world with breathlessness and the scent of aloes and leaves and moss and he felt if she was sitting there beside him he would be glad to dead too.

VICTORY AND THE BLIGHT

Victory didn't even good open his barbershop when Brown reach to play draughts, with him a stringy bushyhead fellar who Victory see once or twice about the town. Right away Victory face changed. To have draughts playing in the barbershop before he began working was sure to blight him for the rest of the day. And to make it worse, the fellar with Brown was a stranger. As he was thinking how to tell this to Brown, Pascal came in and sat down for a trim. Though now, technically, he was about to work, Victory still had this feeling that Brown and his pardner bring with them a blight to his barbershop this Saturday morning.

'The draughts board underneath the bench,' Victory said, with stiff aloofness, not even looking at Brown. 'When you finish with it, put it back where you get it.'

Brown didn't even hear him, he was so busy introducing the pardner who had come in with him. 'This fellar new up here. He working on the farm, with Walker and Carew and them.'

Victory looked at the fellar, not wanting to appear to be interested.

'My name is Ross,' the newcomer said. 'From Arima.'

'And the man you looking at,' said Brown,' is the great Victory. If you want to get the run of this town, stick close to him. Sports, fete, woman, Victory is the boss.' Pointing to the photographs on the wall, Brown added, 'You see him there on the wall? Tell me which one you think is him?'

The fellar named Ross stood before the photographs, cut out from magazines and framed and his eyes went over Joe Louis and Jack Johnson and Sugar Ray Robinson and Mohammed Ali, and over the West Indies cricket team with Worrell and Weekes and Walcott and Sobers and Hall and they came down to the Wanderers cricket team, the team with Rupert and Manding and Hailings and Slim and Cecil and the Ramcharan brothers and to Penetrators football team with Berris and Mervyn and Campbell and Bass and Jacko and Breeze, and then he pointed to a photograph with Victory in a blazer, standing in the back row of the Wanderers team.

'That is the year they went to Tobago,' Brown said in a kind of glee. 'And that one,' he said pointing to the photograph of a young muscular fellar on a rostrum receiving a trophy from a middle-aged white woman, 'Tell me, who that is?'

'That is you?' the fellar named Ross asked.

'Fifteen years ago,' said Victory. 'Victor ludorum. Hundred, two hundred, long jump, high jump. That is the Warden wife giving me the prize.'

'Didn't know he was an athlete too, eh,' Brown said gleefully. 'I tell you the man is everything.'

Slightly appeased Victory took up the cloth to put around Pascal's neck to keep the hair off his clothes. He shook it out, flop, flop, flop, went around behind Pascal and fit it over him, then he pinned the cloth at Pascal's neck. Brown, in the meantime, had picked up the draughts board and was moving out the bench so he and his pardner could sit astraddle for their game.

'And don't block the door,' Victory said. 'And that bench. One of the legs ready to fall off. People sit down on that bench like they riding a horse.'

Brown and his pardner were setting up the knobs.

'Wait,' Victory said. 'You better wait 'till I start to trim this head before you move a knob. I really don't want a blight to fall on me today.'

'Okay, chief,' the fellar named Ross said.

'Chief?' Victory looked directly at him. 'I thought Brown tell you my name.'

'Okay, Victory,' the fellar named Ross said.

Victory had his scissors at ready; but, now, Pascal was fiddling with the cloth pinned at his neck. 'If it too slack,' Victory cautioned, 'hair will get on your skin.'

'Too tight,' Pascal said.

Without another word Victory unpinned the cloth, slackened it and pinned it again. Somehow he felt today wasn't going to be his day.

'How you want your trim?' he asked, clicking his scissors over Pascal's ear.

'Clean it,' Pascal said.

Victory paused, 'Think a clean head will suit you?' Then, he chuckled, 'Look at the nice head this man have to take a good trim and he telling me clean it.' He chuckled again, the chuckle turning to a smile, the smile widening his lips, swelling his face, 'Like you want to put me out of business. Like you want me to leave this trade and go and drive taxi or something.' He clicked his scissors again, faster this time, 'Clean it, you say?'

'Okay. Trim me how you want,' Pascal said. 'My head is in your hands.' He was laughing too.

'Trim you how I want?' Victory stopped his scissors. 'I can't do that. Your head is not my head. I here to do as the customers say. If you say clean, is clean. I would clean it.' A seriousness was creeping into his voice, 'Look, I have one of those machines here that you could just plug in ... they call it a clipper. I could just plug in the clipper and put it on your head and bzzz! Just like that, and all your hair gone. But, I don't call that barbering. Barbering is playing music. Everything have to flow. Things have to fit.'

'Victory, just give me a good trim, not too low,' Pascal said, trying with a light tone to ease the heaviness of the mood he felt descending.

Victory started his scissors clicking again, but did not touch it to Pascal's head, 'No. Serious. I mean it. I could just plug in that machine, that clipper and put it on your head, and you will give me the same three dollars and bzzzz! Your head will be clean.' He touched the scissors to Pascal's hair, 'Everything in the world losing taste, everything quick, quick, quick.... And you know how I get this clipper? A pardner send it from the States for me. The latest. You know who send it? Rupert, the fast bowler from Wanderers. He gone up there in the States and see this clipper and he say, "Victory will like this" and he send it for me.'

'How long he away now?' Pascal asked.

'Four, five years. Last time I hear about him he was living in New Jersey. I always wonder why he send me the clipper.'

'Maybe he didn't like how you used to trim him,' Brown said.

After the laughter, the barbershop was filled with the sound of the clicking scissors, with Brown and the fellar named Ross intent on their game.

'Those was the days when Wanderers was Wanderers,' Brown said. 'This barbershop was the centre. On a Saturday morning you couldn't get in. All the young teachers and civil servants lined up to talk cricket and boxing and waiting to trim. Those days real draughts used to play, with Castillo and Cecil and Mr Arthur leaving Libertville to clash with Paul. Now Paul, too, gone away.'

'The worst thing this government do is to allow people to go away,' Victory said. And he swung the barbering chair around to get to tackle the other side of Pascal's head.

Tugging at the cloth pinned loosely at his neck, Pascal held up a hand to stop Victory, 'You know this thing kinda slack.'

'Hair scratching your skin,' Victory said with undisguised triumph, and began to unpin the cloth once more. 'Pascal, you know what wrong with you. You always feel it have an easy way in everything. Some things aint have no short cut. You just have to do them. No short cut,' he said, tightening the cloth at Pascal's neck, and pinning it.

Suddenly there was an uproar from the draughts game. 'Come and see how this man dead and he don't know! Come and see play!' Victory couldn't believe it. It was the fellar named Ross making this big uproar. The first time this man step into my barbershop, and not even for a hair cut and hear the noise he making, Victory thought, stopping his barbering to allow Pascal to see the position of the game.

Brown countered well, they swapped a few knobs and the tension eased. Victory clicked his scissors and Pascal settled back in the chair.

'So, Victory, what is going to happen to your side now?' Pascal asked, idly. With Victory working on the front of his head, he was looking at the photographs on the wall.

'Which side?' Victory answered.

'You know who I mean, Wanderers. Your side.'

'Wanderers is not a side. Wanderers is a club. A club is not a side. A side is when you pick up eleven fellars to play a match and next week you have to look to pick up eleven fellars again. A club is solid. It is something to belong to.'

'What going to happen to your club when all your players gone away?'

'All? All the players?'

'Well, the stars. Prince, your fast bowler going to Canada. Murray going. Ali gone to the States.'

'Who else going?' Victory asked. He didn't like this talk.

'Is your club. You should know.'

'What you want us to do? They going to study. They have to think about their future. They have to get their education. Just now, just from the fellars who leave and go away from Cunaripo and they come back with their BAs and MAs and Ph dees they could run the government.'

'I wish I was one of them going,' Brown said. He was relaxed now. Ross had miscalculated.

Victory was ready now to clean the edges of Pascal's head with the razor. Quickly, he lathered the shaving brush and brushed it across the edge of hair he was going to remove, then, tilting the chair, bending at the knees, he swept the razor in brisk, deft strokes at the base of Pascal's head and behind his ears, nobody saying anything, Pascal sitting very still.

Then Victory attacked the head once more with the scissors; then, with a powder puff, he puffed some white powder over the places where he had wielded the razor. He took up a comb and handed it to Pascal. He was going to do the final shaping of the hair now.

'Comb out your hair,' he said to Pascal. 'Wait. Is so you does comb your hair?' he asked, seeing Pascal combing from back to front.

'I combing it *out*. I usually comb it backwards.'

'Well, comb it backwards, just as you does comb it when you dollsing up.' Watching Pascal comb his hair, Victory continued talking. 'You build a club to last, to stand up. They say nothing can't last in Cunaripo. They say we can't build nothing. And you build a club and next thing you know, bam! fellars you building it with gone away.'

'What you want them to do?' Pascal asked.

'You think I going to stay here just to play cricket?' Brown said.

'*Just?*' Victory asked. '*Just* to play cricket? How you mean *just* to play cricket? What you think put us on the map, make us known in Pakistan, England, Australia? You all don't know what to care about?'

'You have to be able to afford to care,' Brown said. 'How you expect a fellar like me scrambling for a living, to care about cricket?'

'And how you will care about anything? Somebody will pay you to care? They will give you money and then you will care, eh, Brown? Money will make you care?' Victory had stopped work on Pascal's head.

'I would go away to better my position,' Brown said. 'Not because I don't care.'

'Betterment? By the time you come back you stop playing cricket, you seeing 'bout wife and children, you get fat. It was like if you was never here. Sometimes I look through the scorebook and see the names of players who used to play: Bridges, Kedar, Housen, Francis, Lee, Bisson, Griffith. Was like they was never here. Maybe the government should give a subsidy to care, eh, Brown, eh?'

'Is not the going away,' the fellar named Ross said.

Victory turned upon him, 'Is not the going away? Wait!
You come in this barbershop a stranger and making more
noise than anybody and now you telling me "is not the going
away"?'

'Is not the going away,' Ross said, holding his ground in the
now silent barbershop, 'What it is? Is what they do while they
here …. I see Housen. I see him play in Arima and I see him
play in 'Grande. I remember him like today, and is how long
ago I see him play? He bring an excitement, a magic, a life.
You see him on the field and you see life. You see yourself. Is
like that, I miss a man like Housen. I glad he was here.'

The silence deepened in the barbershop.

'Is true, Victory,' Pascal said. 'I play against him once. He
playing for Dades Trace, I playing for Colts, and when he
finish bat … I mean, when we at last get him out, the whole
field was clapping, not because we out him, because of the
innings he play. Is true. The man coulda bat.'

Victory spun the chair around and crouched and looked at
Pascal's head, then he spun the chair again and looked at the
head as a surveyor looking for an angle. Then he rose up.

'So you does play cricket?' Victory asked, turning now to
the fellar named Ross, his scissors clicking once again. 'What
you do? Bat? Bowl?'

'Open bat and bowl medium pace. Inswing mostly, but
now and again I does get one to move away.'

'Ross, you say your name is? From Arima. It had a fellar
used to work with the electricity company. Gerome Ross. Tall,
kinda good looking, always with his hair cut neat and his
moustache trimmed?'

'Gerome? That is my first cousin.'

'When he was up here, he was my good pardner. Neat,
clothes always sharp, dressed to kill when he playing cricket,
but he couldn't play fast bowling. Bounce one at him and he
start to dodge away. Rupert used to have him hopping. What
about him?'

'He get kinda fat,' Ross said.

Victory looked down at his own middle, 'Just now I have to start some jogging. Or maybe start to referee some football. Pascal, you don't remember Gerome? Coulda kick a football *hard*. Goalies used to cry when they see him coming.'

Brown had been studying the draughts board and now, as if he had the whole game worked out, he pushed a knob and said to Ross, 'Your play.'

Victory finished touching up Pascal's head, went around behind him and unpinned the cloth, taking it off carefully so that the hair wouldn't fall on Pascal's clothes. He brushed the tufts of cut hair off the cloth into a heap on the floor, then went to the door and holding the cloth with two hands dusted it out, flap, flap, flap, then he began to fold it. When he turned it was to see Pascal standing in front the mirror looking at his head admiringly.

'You still think I shoulda clean it?' Victory asked, still folding the cloth.

Pascal turned his head this way and that. Then a smile broke onto his face, 'How much I have for you?'

'The price aint gone up, Victory said.

As Pascal put his hand in his pocket, Brown let out a big exclamation and slapped a knob down on the draughts board, same time springing to his feet just as the legs of the bench gave away, upsetting the whole game, but not before Ross, with a quickness that amazed Victory, had leapt from the falling bench. Victory thinking, yes, he's an opening bat in truth.

'I tell you,' Victory said sternly. 'I tell you the legs of that bench not good. I don't have money to pay compensation when somebody break they back. People sit down on that bench like they riding a horse. Brown,' he said, his tone changing, 'You better come tomorrow with your hammer and fix that bench before somebody get kill.'

Ross had moved to the mirror and was looking at his head. Then he lowered himself into the barbering chair, 'You think you could give me a trim, Victory? I does really trim in Arima, but I going to be up here now.'

140

'How you want it?' Victory asked, picking up the cloth once again.

'Now,' said Ross. 'It mustn't be too low. Cut down the sides, level off the back, and leave my muff.'

Victory unfolded the cloth, went to the doorway and dusted it out, flop, flop, flop, then he came around behind Ross to pin the cloth around his neck, 'And, you know,' Victory said as he drew the ends of the cloth securely around Ross' neck, 'When you step through that door this morning, I sure you was a blight.'